THE BLACK CROW BOOK OF BEST NEW HORROR

VOLUME 1

A Black Crow Books original

The acknowledgements on page 249 constitute an extension of this copyright page

Published in Great Britain 2025 by Black Crow Books Limited

ISBN 978-1-80553-008-4 (Hardback)

Printed and bound by CPI Group (UK) Ltd,
Croydon, CRO 4YY

blackcrowbooks.co.uk

CONTENTS

INTRODUCTION 1

IT GETS EVERYWHERE LISA TUTTLE 7

DROP SHOCK ALLY WILKES 23

MUSES LILY KADE 47

GHOST HUNT ADRIAN TCHAIKOVSKY 65

THE MIDNIGHT BURN TL HUCHU 85

THE BUTCHER OF PUCKLEY VILLAGE V CASTRO 103

TELL ME I'M SCRUMPTIOUS OLIVIE BLAKE 119

THE COMPENSATION RAMSEY CAMPBELL 141

THE OTHER BROTHER RIAN HUGHES 159

STAY IN TOUCH LINDY RYAN 181

MR PERFECT SUSI HOLLIDAY 195

BOW KNEE LAKE TIM LEBBON 207

BACKSLIDING CLAY MCLEOD CHAPMAN 223

INTRODUCTION

Horror is booming. You really can't escape it. Horror films are topping the box office, genre publishing is growing exponentially, theme park rides have been inspired by franchises, and horror nostalgia is back. The genre is metastasizing and terrorizing the world, giving birth to fucked up sub-genre horror babies coming to give you night terrors or insomnia-driven existentialism.

The worst horror is simply turning on the news, of course. I'm deciding here to focus on make-believe; the genre itself, which at its best, allows us to turn the lens on our society, examine our deepest fears that fester in the darkest recesses, bring them into broad daylight where we can study them, take their power away. All while telling an emotionally involving, exciting, scary story. I hope you'll find that within these pages.

My publishing career started in 2010. Two weeks into my first role, I attended my first World Horror Convention, and the launch of *The Mammoth Book of Best New Horror*, edited by Stephen Jones. I couldn't have asked for a better introduction to the horror book community. The title of this collection also pays homage to the aforementioned series.

Fifteen years later, I'm having another 'pinch me' moment. My younger Point Horror-loving self could never imagine I'd go from hiding at family gatherings with my beaten-up paperbacks to, well, hiding at family gatherings reading horror stories I've published. Indoor cats unite!

I'm both proud and honoured to have worked with some of the very best authors in genre fiction. As a result, I've been able to invite some of those authors to join our inaugural anthology. It's a huge privilege to have such an eclectic and diverse mix of fabulous authors on board and I want to thank each of you for agreeing to be a part of this passion project. Your support means more than you could ever know. An extra shoutout to contributor Rian Hughes who also designed our fabulous logos and cover art for this collection. Thank you for your patience and guidance to help create something truly unique.

Thank you to Matt Holland for putting your trust in me, and to Sean Preene for calming the storm. To Martyn Waites for being my editorial support, sounding board and personal cheerleader.

Finally, and most importantly, I want to thank you, my dear fellow Horror Nerd, for picking up this book of the bizarre. For supporting indie publishers, booksellers, and the horror community. One of us.

Jamie xx
Publisher, Black Crow Books
Got a question? Email us hello@blackcrowbooks.co.uk

IT GETS EVERYWHERE

LISA TUTTLE

It was in his mouth: something that did not belong in a ham sandwich.

Gingerly, hoping he was imagining it, fooled by a bit of gristle, he removed the damp, crumbling first bite from his mouth, and peeled off the top layer of bread. He was not wrong. There it lay, straggling across the pink meat dotted with yellow mustard: one long, dark hair.

Not his. His thinning hair was short and a pale noncolour she called 'mousey' and stroked like he was her pet.

She was gone. He was alone in his house, and he'd made the sandwich himself, from a loaf of sliced supermarket white and ham from a sealed packet. Not for a moment did he imagine the hair had come from the head of a factory worker. He knew it too well.

He threw the sandwich in the bin and set about making a fresh pot of coffee. While he waited for it to brew, he walked into the lounge and stood by the French windows, staring out at the garden through steadily falling rain, remembering her slovenly ways. The way she never properly cleaned the bath, but left her long black hairs adorning the sides, or clumped together blocking the drain. Alternatively, she let them swirl away with the water and shrugged it off when the sink backed up, leaving him with the filthy job of clearing the pipes. If he complained, she would point out that this was *his* house, and the problem was caused by the build-up of soap, toothpaste, and shaving cream, not just her hair. The long hair that he loved, or so he said. Hadn't he begged her not to cut it? Their arguments usually ended with him in the wrong.

Despite their spats, he loved her, and now he missed her with an ache he was sure would never end.

Everything he touched or looked at reminded him of her. Those rose bushes in the garden: she had bought them, like a promise she would stay. She had even cleared a space for them, but never got around to planting them. He'd had to do that for her, knowing she would never see them in bloom.

Outside, the rain fell even more heavily, but it was tears that blurred his vision now, filling his eyes in an unstoppable flood of grief.

He dreamed of her again that night; a miserable dream that was little more than a relentless replay of their last arguments.

It was the problem that had loomed over their relationship from the start: she was a foreign national on a temporary work visa. She had a good job in the NHS. She was needed. Nobody there wanted her to leave, and she had hoped to be granted the right to remain, but it had been a wan hope. Recent changes to immigration laws had put the final nail in it: she didn't make enough money to live here, and the time was fast approaching when she would have to go.

That didn't mean back to Poland. As an EU citizen, she could travel to any country in the EU and stay as long as she liked. He didn't share her freedom of movement, but he could visit her and vice versa. His argument was that they did not have to break up. If she could find a job in France, or the Netherlands, or Ireland, it would be easy to get together fairly often and they'd text and speak every day. Lots of couples managed such relationships.

She was contemptuous of his plan, saying that it sounded like the most expensive and long-drawn-out way to end a love affair she'd ever heard of. Either they stayed together or admitted it was over. If he loved her, he would go with her.

But that was as hopeless a dream as hers had been of being allowed to stay. Even if he married her, she could be deported. And if he went abroad, he could expect to be kicked out after six months.

She countered that the European nations accepted the human right to family life and did not wilfully separate people who loved each other and lived together—especially if they were married.

As calmly as he could, he made the case that he would still be unemployable in any country where he did not speak the language, and even in Ireland he thought it unlikely he would be able to get any work as satisfying and as well-paid as what he did now. He was willing to start looking for any opportunities, but he couldn't encourage her to hope.

She wondered why he couldn't keep his job, just do it from another country – 'Why not? It is mostly online, no? And they already let you work from home three days a week.'

But they insisted that all employees show up, in the office, in the flesh, a minimum of two days a week. If he pushed for more it would win him no concessions, he was certain. If he pushed too hard, insisted that he could do it all entirely remotely, they might just let him go. It was not a job he could afford to lose. That gave him a better idea – better than living apart. He made enough to support them both. Once her job ended, why shouldn't she stay? Without a job, without asking for benefits, why would she need to prove she had the right to be here? If she kept her head down, it would be like she'd disappeared, as far as officials were concerned.

She'd glared at him, furious. She would not be disappeared! She would not be 'kept.' She was no little housewife. And she was no illegal immigrant. How could he ask her to break the law, to hide, never to go abroad again? No work, no holidays, never to see her mother again… He said he loved her, so why not prove it? Take a chance. If he sold this house there would be enough money to fund a new life *together* somewhere else. He was smart, he'd find another job, or, better, he could freelance or even start his own business.

He was shocked by how much she asked of him. It was too much. She was asking him to give up everything, his every claim to security: his job, his home which was also his only asset, inherited from his grandparents; everything he knew – for what? Her fantasy of life in a foreign country where somehow everything would work out for the best, for both of them? No. He wouldn't do it. She was asking him to sacrifice everything.

For once, she did not respond with anger, but only a sad resignation, saying softly, 'I think you love your house more than me.'

In the morning, as he stood under the shower, he felt water gathering in the tub around his feet. By the time he was finished, it was up to his ankles, and did not subside even when he turned off the shower. He crouched and ran a finger around the little plastic insert over the plughole. He could have sworn he'd checked and found it clean before he stepped under the shower, but when he raised his hand he saw a sodden swirl of hair.

He got out of the tub and wrapped the tiny nest in a square of toilet paper, then dropped it into the toilet, but it made no difference: the water did not even start to drain. He remembered that, just as she rarely bothered to clear out the hair the insert collected, she never washed the thing itself. Over time, a skin of soap scum built up – too much to be rinsed away. The drain cover must be removed and scrubbed on both sides with a stiff brush before it was replaced.

Plunging his hand into the water, he found the edge of the insert and pried it free.

Nothing changed. The water remained still, and too murky for him to see the problem. He reached in again and groped.

Fingers met a soft, yielding mass, closed on it and pulled. He was still tugging even as his hand came out of the water and he saw it was filled with hair. Still more came up as he continued to pull, staring in disbelief – how much more could there be?

At last, the welcome gurgle of water told him the pipe was clear. He stared at the disgusting mass of hair and wondered what to do with it. His instinct was to flush it away, but what if it blocked the toilet? The image of it lingering, becoming a net to catch his own shit, made him shudder, so he shoved it into the small, lidded wastebin that was one of her few contributions to their home: the rest were cushions, candles, and kitchen gadgets he didn't need.

From another room came the song of his phone. He paused long enough to shrug into his bathrobe, then rushed to answer. And wished he had not, because it was one of her friends, wanting to know where she was and why her many texts and voicemails went unanswered.

'I couldn't tell you. She's not here. She didn't tell you? Well, she left me. I don't know. I don't think she's coming back...maybe, maybe she will but... France, I think. I told you, I don't know. It's over. She left me. What? Her phone? How should I know? She blocked me. Maybe she has a new number. Well, maybe you're not quite as important to her as you…sorry. Yeah. Right. Bye.'

He didn't think she'd contact him again. He thought about blocking her number but rejected the idea. Now in a thoroughly bad mood, he went into the kitchen and made a pot of coffee on autopilot, unwanted memories crowding in.

Their last quarrel had not been about anything important. In fact, it was completely stupid, and if only they'd both managed to keep their tempers it need not have blown up the way it did.

It began with a problem with the vacuum cleaner. He'd been doing the lounge carpet, as per usual, while she started her day off by lounging around still undressed – in his bathrobe – scrolling through videos or messages on her phone and giggling while she waited for her hair to dry enough for the next stage of self-care: application of product, hot comb, and blow-dry. He'd discovered that the brushes on the machine were so snarled up in long black hairs that they could not rotate. Unravelling the mess was a struggle. Her giggling annoyed him, and finally he lashed out, calling her a lazy, dirty bitch.

Of course it was unfair, and his anger was misdirected, but she was even worse than he was – the phrase 'hair trigger' applied to her temper, and once it had been set off, there was hell to pay.

He knew as soon as he spoke that a huge row was inevitable. Maybe, in a way, he'd even wanted it, to clear the tension between them and allow them to come together again.

But it escalated so quickly, as she came at him, her claws out, and it was a more violent clash than ever before. He might shout or say nasty things, but he had never struck a woman in his life. It was how he had been raised. She, of course, had no such scruples and, when she felt words – perhaps especially English words – were not strong enough to express her displeasure, she never hesitated to slap him. Knowing this, he could usually dodge the worst of her blows, but when that wasn't enough, he had to restrain her. Then it was her turn to dodge and evade him, while still trying to land a kick or a slap, and a strange, ungainly dance ensued.

He stopped his thoughts right there, poured the coffee, topped it up with milk, and took it into the lounge to sit and drink it in comfort until it was time to get dressed and be at his 'work station', otherwise known as the kitchen table.

Still unsettled by the phone call and the memories it had aroused, he trembled, and as he raised the cup to his lips, a splash of milky coffee landed on his bare chest and partly on the lapel of his bathrobe.

Swearing, he set the cup down carefully and fumbled in his pocket, hoping that the lump he could feel there was a tissue, but when he pulled it out, he saw more of her hair.

So much hair.

He could visualise her so clearly, seated in this very armchair, wrapped in the same bathrobe (she preferred his thick terry robe to her own skimpy kimono-style wrap), combing her fingers through her long, lustrous hair. Every swipe of her hand garnered a harvest of loose hairs, making him wonder how anyone could lose so much hair every day without ending up with bald patches. She rolled her eyes and told him not to be an idiot.

When she combed her hair with her fingers like that, a peaceful, serious expression on her face, she would pause to roll the gathered hairs together, twining them around her fingers into something that reminded him of a video he had seen of traditional hand-weaving methods, spinning a sheep's fleece into yarn to be knitted or woven into woollen clothing.

She did nothing useful with the yarn she made of her own

hair; when she was done, she wound it up into a ball to be thrown away. More often than not, she'd leave it 'just for now' on the nearest convenient surface or tuck it away in her pocket – usually *his* bathrobe pocket.

Not that he minded her wearing his things. He loved the sight of her wrapped up in one of his shirts or in this bathrobe that still held traces of her sweet clean scent. The familiar smell rose from her hair and stirred him profoundly. How he missed her.

The ache of tears was in his throat. He shoved the hairball back into his pocket and lurched to his feet. Time was passing. He had to get to work.

Halfway to the door, on his way to the bedroom, a sudden pain in his left foot turned his easy stride into a hop-along hobble. He didn't know what had happened and was wary of making it worse: had he stepped on something, cut his toe, or was it a cramp?

He dropped onto the bed and grabbed his foot, lifting it for a closer inspection. He saw no sign of injury, but his big toe throbbed. Probing and peering, he discerned something at the base of the toe: there was a thin, dark line.

It was a hair, wrapped so tightly around his toe it had become a tourniquet cutting off the flow of blood. How could that happen? Could the hair have fallen into a natural loop, become a miniature lasso lying hidden in the thick grey carpet, just the right size for his toe to enter before it tightened like a noose?

It was really hurting now. Fine as it was, he felt it biting into his flesh like a cheesewire. Was that blood he saw? Was he really about to lose a toe?

He scratched at it desperately but could not get a grip: his nails were too blunt, and the hair was too fine, too deeply embedded in his flesh.

There had to be a way; he needed something to cut it. But

scissors were too big, and he didn't have a razor blade. Then he remembered her manicure set and hobbled into the bathroom to search the cabinet. Yes, it was there, and inside a pair of scissors with slender, sharp curved blades. For a wonder, despite his pain and fear, his hands did not shake. Propping his bare foot on the toilet, he used one hand to isolate and steady the toe, the other to manoeuvre the scissors, and managed on his third attempt to slide the tip of one blade under the hair. He felt a slight sting, then the hair snapped, and he was free.

Swallowing a sob of relief, he rubbed his toe and felt it come back to life. He must have imagined the blood; the only damage he could see was a slight scratch from the scissors. Now that it was over, he was ashamed of his overreaction. How could he have thought a human hair was enough to sever a toe?

He was soaked with sweat. He would need another shower before he got dressed. But no—he decided it was more important to do whatever he could to get rid of every hair she'd left behind. He generally kept the house tidy, and he thought he had done a good job with a thorough clean of the lounge already, but evidently he had not done enough. The clear plastic bin of the Dyson quickly filled, and while some of it was the usual dust and detritus that would accumulate in any household, the major part was hair. Somehow, those long, dark hairs of hers had managed to evade capture by lurking in corners, stuck to the furniture, tangled in the carpet, but no more.

He vacuumed twice, swept and mopped and dusted every room, changed the sheets, did another load of laundry, all thoughts of work forgotten until he paused for a bite to eat, and checked his messages. His absence from work had been noted. He hastily concocted an apology, claiming he had been too ill even to get out of bed and grab his phone until now.

Once he'd marked himself as absent due to illness for the rest of the day, he realised he really didn't feel very well. Too much paranoia, fear, and housework had nearly done him in. He finished his bread and cheese and collapsed into bed.

He woke from a deep and dreamless sleep to a choking sensation.

Something was caught in his throat. He could neither swallow it nor cough it up.

He reared up in bed, clutched at his chest and struggled to breathe. He was in his own bed, and from the light he guessed it was late afternoon, but he had no memory of why he'd been sleeping at such a time.

At last, he felt something shift inside his chest, and his next cough brought it up. He was forced to bend at the waist as he vomited a substantial mess into his duvet-covered lap. It looked like wet strands of kelp or grass – nothing he could imagine ever having eaten – and then he heaved again, ejecting even more of the stuff.

Hair. It was hair. *Her* hair was somehow inside him, and now it was forcing its way out, gagging him, erupting from his mouth and dripping from his nose. It soon began to ooze out from the other end, too.

Impossible, but he felt it, knew it was true. More of her hair inside him than there could ever have been on his late girlfriend's head. It was growing inside his body and under his skin, filling every hollow, wrapping tightly around each and every organ, penetrating his bones, until there was no room for anything else; squeezing his lungs until he could no longer breathe, squashing his heart until it ceased to beat.

The pain was incredible, horrific, but only for as long as he was alive to feel it. Soon he was beyond pain. He was transformed, and there was nothing of him left, nothing that was not made of her hair. Only a dead thing in the shape of what had once been a human being.

ABOUT THE AUTHOR

LISA TUTTLE began her career as a published writer in the early 1970s, and won the John W. Campbell Award for Best New Science Fiction Writer of the year in 1974. She's the author of seven novels and more than a hundred short stories. Born and raised in Texas, she has lived in a remote, rural part of Scotland for the past twenty-five years. Her first novel, *Windhaven*, was a collaboration with George R. R. Martin published in 1981. This was followed by a horror novel, Familiar Spirit, in 1983. Unable to stick to one well-defined genre, although most of her work features elements of horror and/or dark fantasy, she went on to write novels of psychological suspense (*Gabriel and The Pillow Friend*), science fiction (*Lost Futures*), and contemporary/mythic fantasy (*The Mysteries and The Silver Bough*) as well as books for children and young adults, and non-fiction (*Encyclopedia of Feminism and Heroines*).

Short stories were her first love, and remain important. Her first short story collection, *A Nest of Nightmares*, was published in the U.K. in 1986, and two years later featured in *Horror: 100 Best Books* edited by Stephen Jones and Kim Newman. Her other collections include *A Spaceship Built of Stone and other stories* (1987), *Memories of the Body: Tales of Desire and Transformation* (1992), *Ghosts and Other Lovers* (2002), and *Objects in Dreams* (2012). A number of her short stories have appeared in 'best of the year' anthologies and been nominated for awards; *Closet Dreams* won the 2007 International Horror Guild Award. She edited an influential anthology of horror stories by women writers, *Skin of the Soul*, first published in 1990.

DROP SHOCK

ALLY WILKES

With apologies to my favourite reality TV show

A yawning pit opened up in Tom's stomach. Excitement? Anticipation? He didn't know – but it made him dizzy. With the helicopter blades snick-snicking through the air overhead, the nearby pines bent back like fugitives from some nuclear blast, and the thin scrubby grass of the Canadian wilderness shook around him. Tom could feel the pressure beating inside his own ribcage, telling him that he was here at last.

I'm on the show.

Holy shit, I'm on the show.

Craning his neck and shading his eyes, Tom watched the departing helicopter as it became a speck in the white-grey sky. The trees below him gave one last shudder before standing upright again, and ripples formed on the lake in great concentric circles, following the aircraft out of sight. Tom had played this moment in his head a thousand times – had watched and re-watched this particular reality TV show as if it was his personal bible.

He needed to set up his camera, get a good shot of himself as he stood on the hilltop, fists raised. A triumphant yell piercing the September air: *Here I am.*

One hundred days!

He repeated the show's name, like a mission statement, as he turned on the spot to get his bearings. Up here, the trees were few and stunted – and he was completely alone, the helicopter a memory. He was a dot on the shores of the lake, small and isolated, ready for one hundred days' worth of lone survival. Just him against the wilderness.

Something stopped him, though, from setting up the camera to take that all-important establishing shot. The wide grin on his face felt wrong, a little too forced, as if he were trying to show the landscape his teeth. It was a cold day – *and colder to come!* – with the promise of rain lurking in that blackening sky. Tom wrapped his arms around himself, feeling oddly vulnerable all of a sudden. He needed to set up shelter, start on making a fire.

When it got dark, predators would be a problem.

'Please be careful,' his wife had pleaded. He could see her now, rose-lit in the kitchen, sleeves rolled up as she fussed with something in the oven. 'I don't like the thought of you being in bear country unarmed.'

'I'll have my bow.' Not that he was confident using the unwieldy hunting bow – not yet. But the show's rules prohibited firearms, and he'd lain awake at night grinding his teeth over it.

'That's not–'

'What?' he'd snapped. 'Don't you think I can handle myself? Shit, you've seen some of the losers they've had on there…'

Her bottom lip had trembled. He'd softened, taken her into his arms; she smelled of cinnamon. 'Don't you worry about me. Everyone comes back. Even the girls.'

Tom looked around the barren landscape, the way the tree line established itself like a solid barrier down the slope a hundred yards away. Visibility was poor. He repeated the thought to himself as he bent to haul his equipment under shelter he could find: *Everyone comes back, even the girls.*

Everyone loved Casey – no last name needed – with her wide face and friendly grin and gosh-darn-ain't-this-a-hoot attitude. She'd been the winner of the previous season, the only contestant to make it to one hundred days without a catch.

'I dunno,' she said in the post-show interviews, her blue eyes sparkling. 'Plenty of catches!'

And her interviewer had laughed, because her fishing prowess had become an in-joke. By day sixty, she was hauling in long gleaming silver lines of lake trout, slicing them up expertly, her knife flashing in the dying light.

In the TV studio she only looked a touch more polished than in the raw, self-shot footage from the show. Tom had secretly thought she must be packing make-up and a hairbrush, because every day she rolled out of the sleeping bag, she looked put-together in a wholesome, clean-faced way that sent him wild. She'd seemed to get even sunnier as the months rolled on, as the other contestants starved and set their shelters on fire and got small accidental wounds that – inevitably – turned bad.

How do I get a girl like that? he'd thought to himself, then glanced at his wife – and felt a pang of guilt. He knew Casey would visit him again in his fantasies, or in the middle of the night. Pink lips, like she bit them – or had smuggled in tinted chapstick.

The studio camera focused in on Casey as she laughed about her time in the wilderness. She used the same phrases she had when she'd been filming herself in mud and grime: *Gotta keep keeping on. It is what it is.* It was oddly soothing, the way she repeated them. As if she didn't have enough words to elaborate.

Drop shock, Tom thought. The former contestants had a name for it: the way your initial plans crumbled in the first few hours alone.

He should have been well on his way to setting up a shelter. But he'd wasted time finding a water source, then going in the opposite direction in search of tinder, then backtracking when he thought he'd found a game trail. Lots of trudging through the dense, wet underbrush of the boreal forest. It was practically night, and he'd gotten turned around, spent a few heart-stopping minutes where he hadn't been sure where he'd left the equipment. One jagged pine looking the same as the next. And now he was sitting on the camera box, staring towards the tree line.

There was something about the trees, when he was in them, that made him deeply uneasy. They were too still. Too silent. How was he going to trap anything out here? The forest seemed determined to hold its breath on him – even the twigs didn't snap underfoot as they should.

It was the utter stillness of the woods he'd always associated with the presence of an apex predator.

And now, looking back down the slope, he could see the faint sway of branches in the wind. Rippling movement. But there wasn't any wind up here on the empty hilltop where he'd been dropped. Just night, falling like a stone.

He thought he caught sight of something –

A flash of purple.

Pale purple – lilac, he thought – the same colour as Casey's waterproof parka. It was unmistakable. It shimmered at the corner of his vision, then disappeared as quickly as it had come.

He'd dropped to his knees without thinking. Making himself smaller, less visible. The stars were coming out, and he cast no shadow on the land. At first, he told himself that maybe she'd left the parka behind: it must be a real shock to the system – the very opposite of drop shock – to be airlifted out after a hundred days alone.

But this wasn't where Casey had camped. Same lake. Different inlet; he'd scoured the maps well in advance. He must be over a hundred miles from where she'd been evacuated.

Drop shock, he thought again. *You're imagining things. Move on.*

A routine became established, as far as one could be. The days were freezing and wet and unpleasant, punctuated by bloodied rabbits and pine-needle stew. Nothing seemed to swim in the dense dark waters of the lake. The nights were worse. Tom lay in his sleeping bag and felt cold and hunger with a violence that startled him.

If Casey could do it…

That was the point, wasn't it? If a girl could do it, so could he.

It was week three before something came sniffing around camp; he'd thought the bears would be bolder, but perhaps they, too, were put off by the horrible stillness of the forest at noontime. The way it seemed to swallow up all sound, even his own voice.

The first sign of the nocturnal intruder was the slow, deliberate, crack of a twig.

Tom sat up in his sleeping bag, heart racing. There was a cold clammy sweat on his forehead; he'd been half-asleep, dreaming of Casey's perfect smile, those even white teeth. He fumbled for his headlamp, and the shelter was illuminated with a cold white light.

He knew what he had to do. He hit record.

'So… yeah. It's probably after midnight and I've just heard a sound outside.'

He wished he had his firearm. The longbow was only good for losing arrows.

He could see his pale face on the camera screen, frozen for

long seconds as he listened for more sounds outside. *Thrilling TV*, he thought dourly, as he tried to filter out the low sound of the waves on the lake and the faint moan of wind on the shore.

Another crack.

'Did you hear that?' He expelled air through his teeth. 'I'm gonna go take a look.'

When he met the cold night air, it stung like a belly-flop into deep water. The darkness was absolute, trees bending to block out the stars. The night-vision function on the camera showed absolutely nothing of use: a series of indistinct, waving white shapes. Trees looked like severed limbs.

Tom hovered in the doorway, pointing the camera.

Crack.

It sounded as though someone had put all their weight, very carefully, onto a branch – and been unlucky.

'Okay, so… there's definitely someone out there.'

He couldn't see shit. If it was a bear, it was being mighty stealthy. And wolves hunted in groups. A wolverine, perhaps? Or a fox.

He didn't know why his mind had gone so quickly to the idea that it was a *someone* – rather than a *something*.

'Huh.' He shut off the camera.

Nothing to see here, folks.

The next morning revealed a small rabbit in the nearest trapline, north-east of the camp, the same direction as those cracked branches. Tom thought about thanking the land, as some of the other contestants did – but screw it, this was *his* trap. He deserved the credit.

He couldn't deny, though, that there was something strange about the kill. The rabbit's neck didn't seem to have caught in the snare wire. There was something… flattened about the little limp corpse. As if it had been hit with a huge stone, then carefully transported to camp. And left for him there.

By day forty, he was certain there was something else out there with him. To combat the feeling, he filmed constantly, talking wherever he went, listening to his words filling up the silence under the trees: the horrible wet dense air that only relented to spit freezing rain or horizontal snow. He talked until his throat was sore, then talked some more.

Once or twice, he thought he might've heard the woods reply.

Nonsense. Dehydration, maybe. Fatigue. Low minerals. Any one of the miserable parasites he might have got from infected food sources (still no fish though, not a single sign of them, and wasn't that weird?). But Tom could've sworn he heard someone *whisper* at him from the trees.

Well, not whisper, perhaps. But it was making a shushing sound.

Urgent, throaty. Low.

And at night, when the sun went down, there started to come the sound of someone whistling: high up on the ridge where the trees parted.

'Okay, you fuckers,' he whispered vehemently to the camera crew he was sure was out there – getting some B-roll footage, perhaps. Winding him up.

He whistled back.

It seemed to encourage them.

When he dreamt about Casey, he saw her two perfect rows of white teeth biting down – *squish* – into a wet fish. The tinkling silver of scales. The slick texture of raw seafood, the way it cleaved, flesh moist and slightly stratified, like the inside of an underripe peach. He watched her throat as she swallowed. It was very pale, and very clean.

How did she keep it so clean, out in the wild? She hadn't come back with half the grime of the other contestants. She still looked like Day One Casey.

Tom was a long way from Day One Tom.

On the appointed day for his wellbeing check, he bared his torso to the camera, getting a good look at himself for the first time in weeks. His ribs stuck out at an angle he wasn't sure was natural. His skin rippled – wrinkled, even – when he pressed a finger into his stomach. His calves were all muscle, his feet blistered and itchy. He'd cut his hair with a knife; wasn't that a staple of the show?

And then – wanting to get a sense of how his wife would see him, when he was back home and they were watching the footage together on the couch after a home-cooked meal – Tom did something he'd been told not to do: he accessed the memory card. Zipped through scenes of him building shelter, maintaining shelter, boiling water, talking to himself, always talking to himself.

Then, his eyes narrowing, he hit pause.

He was on-screen inside his shelter – the pale white light of the headlamp, and the ever-present and ever-claustrophobic pine walls. Crouching beside his fire, which sparked and hissed angrily at the moisture in the air.

He was eating a squirrel.

But that was wrong. Tom had never caught a squirrel.

Tom watched, mesmerised, as he used his teeth to tear meat off the bone. Such a small animal, only a mouthful, but the Tom on camera was clearly enjoying himself, shaking each scrap of meat as though he were a wolf snapping necks. The Tom on camera took a large gulp – as if breathing came second to eating – and looked straight at the camera lens.

He started growling, making deep guttural sounds, bobbing his head up and down. His movements were jerky, uncoordinated.

Tom fumbled to turn the whole thing off. He sat in silence, his heart racing.

He'd never caught a squirrel. They were too fast. They chattered at him, mockingly, from the trees. But there he was, on camera, eating a squirrel on a stick.

Privately, Tom was scared he was losing too much weight. His ribs felt sore, all the time. His muscles twanged and cramped with loss of electrolytes. He entertained – just for a moment – the idea that the wellbeing check might send him home today.

Move on. Don't be a pussy. It ain't over till it's over.

But now there was another problem. Someone who looked just like Tom, who sat in Tom's shelter, used Tom's camera to record himself eating – *but wasn't him.*

Tom wiped the cold sweat from his face, and considered. He needed the money.

He couldn't afford to freak out.

'We're just concerned,' the medic said patiently. He'd probably had media training, or sensitivity training, or some other such bullshit, because his voice never left the same register – quiet, calm, matter-of-fact. The sort of voice that would tell you *sorry, your house is being repossessed.*

'You've lost a lot of weight, but that's not our primary concern here. It's important you understand there wasn't a camera crew here the other night. No-one could have been out here whistling. No-one else has come into your area since the day of the drop.'

'Well maybe I'm hearing things,' Tom mumbled. He meant it as a joke, but the medics exchanged troubled glances – then their eyes slid to the cameraman, who was kneeling some distance from camp, thumbing through the memory cards.

'We've also seen what looks like… worrying behaviour,' the main guy continued.

Tom lifted his chin. 'I don't know what you mean.'

'Some of the footage is pretty troubling. We just need to know you're doing okay. That you're still able to… cope.'

'Look, if this is about the squirrel.' Tom ran his hands through his ugly cropped hair. 'I don't know what to tell you. I was playing it up for the camera. We're meant to entertain, right? Show a little of our wild side. It ain't like we're here for table manners.'

The medics exchanged another look. 'Yes. The squirrel.' There was a pause, and Tom heard the utter stillness of the forest, all around them, leaning in to listen. 'The meat was rotten, Tom. It was rancid. Not fit for human consumption.'

That night, the whistling came closer.

Day sixty-three, and Tom finally learnt how to use his bow. The grouse had been fluttering in and out of the trees all morning, driving him wild and frantic with desire – hunger – need. His hands had shaken so much, it was a wonder he'd managed to get off a clean shot. Then the arc of the arrow through the unnaturally still air. The sound of an indrawn breath – his, someone else's? – and the twang of the arrow finding its target. More muffled struggling. It made ten awkward paces, shuffling and flapping, before Tom caught up with it. Blood gleamed on the snow, crimson and vital, and he took the grouse in both hands. Wrung its neck.

Please, oh please. Give me this one thing.

The blood on his gloves made him think, abruptly, of Casey – Casey the perfect, Casey the winner. Her plump, shiny lips when she'd appeared on the post-show interview circuit. Her skin dewy and moist, cheeks fat like a baby's. No wrinkles, despite her age.

It was as if she'd been born yesterday, made anew in the forest.

Tom could see her, as clearly as if she stood before him. Her small hands. Small cold hands.

His heart was hammering wildly in his chest, and he could taste pennies in the back of his throat. All the hairs were standing up on his arms. Excitement. He realised, with a shudder, that he was hard – that blood was pumping to his groin, that the killing had excited him. Casey's face. Her tiny, even teeth.

It is what it is.

'No,' he said aloud, putting the grouse down and wiping his gloves in the snow. 'I'm not like that.'

Anyone could tell you – he wasn't like that.

His wife was always saying: *You're one of the good ones.*

The trees seemed to say it back at him. The voice sounded like his own.

The next morning, he woke cold and wet in his sleeping bag. Tom thought it was snowfall, that the roof had been penetrated, but with a shiver of sticky familiarity from his teenage days, he eventually realised what had happened. His face rigid with disgust, he used fresh snow to wash off the semen. It dissolved into the land like a mirage.

The weather was too bad to do anything much, so he went through another memory card. It was gloriously mundane, watching himself surviving, listening to himself chatting away for the benefit of the camera. Outside, the trees didn't move in the wind or the rain. Not a single branch seemed to creak. As for small game – forget it.

The silence has to mean something.

The bear was still out there, and Tom knew he had to hunt it. There was no other way. A small damp hollow opened in his heart as he thought of those sleepless nights, lying next to his wife, shit-scared at the thought of coming up on a black bear with nothing but a bow and arrow. He hadn't told her, of course. That wasn't the sort of thing you admitted.

Don't want to worry 'em.

His pops had taught him that.

It is what it is. That's what Casey would say.

Tom watched himself numbly on the little screen, walking along the lake shore, hands in pockets, back to camera. *The show-runners don't like that,* he thought. *Makes for bad TV.*

Then the man on camera turned.

'Slow and steady wins the race,' he said, and cracked a wide grin.

What the fuck?

Tom scrambled backwards, wanting to put as much distance as possible between him and that little black box – and the smiling man inside.

Slow and steady.

He'd said it just the other day, on another gloomy afternoon when he'd wandered down to check the lake for signs of life – anything. Skipped a few stones over its depressing surface. Wondered how Casey had managed to charm fish from it, when now, nine months later, there was nothing to be seen. Slow and steady. *Yeah, fuck that.* All an act for the cameras. There was no way he'd have smiled like that, all malice and…

'Teeth,' he whispered. *All malice and teeth.*

It was the *other* Tom. He'd learned to speak.

'You need the food,' he repeated to himself, over and over, as he trudged through wet grass and underbrush up the slopes of the hill. 'You need the money. One hundred days. *One hundred days.*' But his heart was in his mouth, and it all came out garbled. Shit, he didn't know what he'd do if he found the bear. He was badly rattled, worn thin, and didn't know how he was keeping it together. *Don't want to worry 'em.*

'Gotta keep keepin' on,' he muttered. Every crack of a twig seemed to echo through the still landscape, creating the impression of a hundred Toms following him. A hundred grinning impostors.

Move on.

The snow was blowing in his face, that horrible insistent light snow that got into everything, a wet snow that made it difficult for tracks to stick. Still, Tom knelt to look for bear sign. There were a few snapped branches, a low patch of grass that looked like it might've been trampled on. He took that as a good omen, and followed the steadily-vanishing trail uphill. He had maybe half an hour before he wouldn't be able to see shit.

A low cliff face loomed in front of him. There was an opening, a crack between two of the rocks; it looked like it might open out into a proper cave.

Got you, bear.

He didn't want to go in, though. There was something oppressive about the place: the way the sunlight didn't quite make it inside; the moan of the wind as it slalomed off that cliff.

Just a peek. Just a peek, then you can always come back later.

Heart in his mouth, Tom crept up on the opening. Exactly the way his family dog had travelled when hunting – low to the ground, leaving no silhouette. He needed the element of surprise. It came back to bite him, though, when he stuck his head into the small cave mouth.

No bear.

It was a woman.

No – it was Casey. Casey, last season's winner, curled up in a ball like a small animal.

'Is this a fucking joke,' he whispered, more angry than relieved. His voice rising. 'Is this some sort of –'

The words echoed. *Fucking joke.* Came back louder.

He wheeled around, expecting to see a camera crew emerging from the blackness at any minute. But that would be against the rules, wouldn't it? It wasn't day one hundred. Maybe he was the last one out here?

Maybe Casey was here because he'd *won*?

He looked back at the prone woman. Her eyes gleamed, a sliver in the darkness.

Then she was up and on him.

'You've got to stop talking,' she hissed. 'Stop giving it words!'

Her face was close to his own, and her breath *stank.* It smelled of rotting meat and the sweet fruity smell of starvation, the pear undertones that were familiar to every contestant. Tom knew that, if he looked, her teeth wouldn't be white and even. No, they'd be rancid and furry, discoloured from berries and chipped from little pieces of grit. He pushed her away.

No-one could fantasise about *this* girl.

Casey was shockingly thin, and the lines around her mouth had set hard. Her skin was several shades darker than on TV, her face weather-beaten and cracked, and the clothing she wore – that lilac parka, that ridiculous, impractical, no-good-for-hunting parka – was belted with braided shore-grass to stop it falling off her.

Tom thought, with a pang, of the flash of colour he'd seen on his first day out. *Drop shock.*

Had that been… her?

His thoughts stuttered. Had she been here… all along?

'Got any food?' she asked, her voice low and desperate. There was none of the charm of her interviews, or the down-home, folksy demeanour she'd perfected on the show. Tom just stared. 'Man, I could eat a rabbit. Got any rabbit?'

Tom thought about the rabbit that had been left in his trapline – *beaten to death, and left* – and his stomach turned over. He didn't want to think about what sort of creature might have put it there for him, showing a casual self-interest in keeping him alive.

The *other* Tom.

Stop giving it words!

'No,' he managed to get out. 'But I've got grouse. Back at camp.'

'No fish,' she croaked, as if agreeing with him. 'They're spooked by us – or what looks like us.'

'What?'

'You've gotta stop talking all the time. Filming. That was our mistake.' She looked him in the eye, and he could see a burst blood vessel in her own – no longer that piercing baby blue. 'See, we're teaching it how to be us.'

He opened his mouth, but no words came out.

'You've seen it, haven't you? Must have, by now. Coming up on three months, that's when it gets bolder.'

Tom lowered his voice to a whisper, knife-sharp. 'There's something out there pretending to be me.'

She nodded. 'Told ya. I'm famished. Now, how 'bout that grouse?'

Her voice – there was something terribly wrong with it. Whispery, croaky, like a dead thing wheezing through a non-functioning oesophagus. Still, what she was saying made some sort of twisted sense. Tom could taste blood in his mouth.

'What does it want?'

'Oh, you'll see on tap-out day.' Her mouth pulled into a tight hard scowl. 'That's when things will get real nasty.'

I'm not going to tap out.

He nearly said it out loud, but paused, considering. There was something horrifyingly off about this scene, about Casey – so bedraggled, so *wet*, despite the shelter of the cave. She reeked. And when she stood to follow him, he could see she was hobbling, favouring her left leg. A bandage spoke to an old injury. She was teetering, wafer-thin, and dripping. How had she survived? *Everyone comes back, even the girls.* She was just an animal in pain. When she turned to smile at him, her teeth were indeed horrid.

'Whatcha doing?'

'You won't fool me like that,' Tom muttered. 'Won't fool me, won't fool me.' He scrubbed at his hands with a sopping mass of lake-grass, hissing with pain as it scoured the cuts on his palm. Casey had fought –

Teeth and claw, he thought, and –

That wasn't Casey.

Just an animal that needed to be put out of its misery. He'd done the same for their hound, when it got sick, and the veterinarian was too expensive and his wife too soft. He'd done it without saying a word. *Don't want to worry 'em.*

He'd got Casey – the *not-Casey*, the mimic, the Thing – the same way. With a rock, from behind, blood spurting onto his hands and arms. For a tough, dried-up old bird, she'd bled tremendously. But had weighed nothing, nothing at all, when he'd dragged her down to the water, put her into the shallows. Looked at her face one last time, quiet and still and old as the mountains, old as the forests, old as whatever was stalking them out there. Stealing them, one bit at a time.

He'd seen it on camera, hadn't he? The thing which looked like him and acted like him.

Something from out of the trees.

Tom shivered. He was losing daylight. And he was far from his camp, so far he'd have to navigate the dark silent woods by headlamp. He straightened up. Discarded the bloody grass.

Turned the camera on.

The snare came from nowhere, grabbing his leg out from under him.

'Ow, *fuck*!' Tom yelled, his voice too loud in the gathering night. He didn't have to look to know that his ankle was broken. His ankle was broken; he was too far from camp.

And this wasn't his trapline.

The snare was wickedly sharp and tight, far better than one he could make himself.

Well, shit.

Tom was still trying to figure out what to do, hazy with pain, when he heard the *snick-snick* of returning helicopter blades.

'Hey!' he yelled, hobbling to stand. 'Hey, I'm over here!'

But camp was the other side of the hilltop, and that was where the helicopter was landing.

Tom fell to his knees, pressing his hands over his mouth.

No.

The extraction team wouldn't come unless someone pressed the big red button – unless someone gave up, hit the wall, *tapped out.* He screamed uselessly, tugging at the snare wire with his bare hands, cutting up his fingers in the process.

It was cold. *And would get colder still.*

The team were too far away, and his shouts were eaten up by the wind, by the roaring of the helicopter engine, by the waves crashing on the lake, the lake that only Casey (or what was pretending to be Casey) had been able to fish. Her perfect white teeth biting into them, *raw.*

Tom was suddenly more afraid than he'd ever been.

He fought again to stand, nearly blacking out in the process. The wire only squeezed tighter. He screamed into the November air, waving his arms overhead.

'Here I am. Here I am!'

The medics swarmed back to the helicopter, carrying discarded camera equipment. They had one more person with them. One more person, being helped into the waiting aircraft. The TV studio was waiting for Tom – *no last name needed.*

Whatever went back in his place.

It is, Tom thought dizzily – *what it is.*

ABOUT THE AUTHOR

ALLY WILKES grew up in a succession of isolated—possibly haunted—country houses and boarding schools.

After studying law at Oxford, she went on to spend eleven years as a criminal barrister, learning how extreme situations bring out the best (or worst) in human nature.

Ally now lives in Greenwich, London, with an anatomical human skeleton and far too many books about Polar exploration. When she isn't writing or reading horror, she's usually to be found hanging upside-down (like a bat) from her aerial silks.

MUSES

LILY KADE

'Next time, I expect to see a baby.'

I said these words to Maximilian Crane at the height of his fame. One of those over-the-shoulder remarks meant to be jocular, knowing, and just a little bit snide – in other words, a typical goodbye from one writer to another – but in retrospect, I wish I hadn't said anything *but* goodbye.

He was standing at the time in the liminal space between the foyer and his three-laddered library. That library, from the 90s onwards, had been the subject of so many glossy magazine columns that he'd had a special shelf added to hold them all. A self-referential shelf. Or 'shelf-referential' – a joke I'd prepared on the two-hour train journey to Max's secluded northern abode, but forgotten to actually drop into our somewhat one-sided conversation.

Back to what I did say. Max laughed when I said it, one of those legendary, sepulchral laughs that made his expanding belly shake, and his hair (still thick, still mostly sable) fall in punctuation marks across his forehead.

'I'm not a paedophile,' he said.

We had been authors within the same imprint for almost a decade. Our circle of friends overlapped almost to the point of eclipse. I use this word intentionally, because there's no denying that he is – was – the more famous by far. Maximillian Crane, with his awards and his *shelf-referential*. The man the *London Review* had once dubbed 'The Master of Modern Horror' – but I don't need to tell you any more about that. *You* know.

The first invitation came shortly after my second novel, *To the Dust*, came out to modest success. By email – Max had never sent a text message in his life; he was 'ideologically opposed to them'. I was flattered, to say the least. That first visit was what I had expected, perhaps slightly less than I'd hoped, and it set the pattern for the ones that followed, not often, but with a seasonal regularity: pleasant chat, a few drinks, a discussion of our current work, and ending, always, with a rummage through that library. But it was hard not to get the feeling that Max was showing off. The famous writer in his twilight years, benevolently showing his less fortunate successor just how good he'd had it.

And then there were the women.

There was no escaping the conclusion that as Max grew older and fatter – and the shelf of horror novels that bore his name grew longer – and his *name* on those novels grew bigger, until they almost obscured the titles themselves – the women in his life did not grow at all.

Quite the opposite.

On my first visit, he introduced me to May, a tall, shiny-bobbed woman I put in her mid-to-late thirties. On the second, it was Celeste, an art curator with impeccable style who volunteered that she was twenty-nine. Then young Marta, from Poland, who'd left her job as an *au pair* to live with Max; this must not have lasted long, because on the next visit was Isla, whose parents thought she was off on a gap year in Sweden. I'll spare you the rest of the details, because you know the story already. It's the one that never seems to change – the most unoriginal story there is.

'What can I say,' Max said on my last visit, when Vida was out of the room. He raised his hands helplessly. 'They inspire me.'

'They inspire *something* in you,' I said, sipping my Boulevardier.

I was happy to see that Vida, at least, took a no-nonsense approach toward the old man. When he ran his hand down her long, bare legs, she smacked him with a rolled-up copy of his latest puff piece.

'Cancelled!' she said to him, and to me: 'Call the cops, already.'

'Art begets art,' he said grandly, pulling her onto his lap. 'And this is nature's finest artwork.'

Maybe their banter jogged something in me, maybe I was feeling the effects of my recent success (my latest novel had just been optioned), maybe I was still a little jealous of Max, now pushing 60, with his youthful injections of whatever it was that seemed to keep him perpetually in the stratosphere. Or maybe it was the bourbon. Whatever the cause, when I turned at the door an hour later to deliver a parting remark, it came out with a sourness that surprised me.

'Vida's great,' I said, 'but a little old for you, don't you think? You have a reputation to maintain. Next time, I expect to see a baby.'

And to bring the point home, I half-mimicked rocking an infant in my arms.

I was relieved, then, when my usual winter invitation arrived. Not only because it meant my remark hadn't caused a rift, but because Martin, our mutual editor, had been asking me about Max – if I knew how he was, *where* he was, and why he'd stopped replying to emails.

Max answered the door as usual, but instead of his usual excessive warmth, he hung back almost shyly. When he did finally speak he kept his voice low. Quiet. Max was *never* quiet.

Something's wrong. I thought this immediately but dismissed it just as fast. After all, I reasoned, we're all getting older; my own meat suit was beginning to sag in an imitation of sadness. *He's lost some weight, damn him.* But Max was diminished in more than a physical way, his enormous presence dimmed to barely a flicker.

As I disinterred myself from the tomb of my winter coat, I filled the silence with chatter. News from our mutual friends, my latest book review (in the *Sunday Times*, no less!), who had gotten wasted at the Poe Prize 'Winners Passed and Present' dinner.

As if by instinct, I looked around for the girl. As if answering my instinct, she stepped into the centre of the room. Directly into the strong winter sunlight that fell in a long, skinny square across her eyes, though she didn't blink or squint. Those eyes, a startling blue, stayed wide open in her milk-white face, which paled against her even whiter hair – an ageless face, I thought, one that had definitely not seen more than eighteen or twenty turns. A face that still bore the faint red craters of teenage acne – but was nevertheless not *young*, not by any mortal understanding of that word.

'This is Friday,' said Max from somewhere behind me. He sounded far away.

'Friday?'

'Frida,' she corrected, in a deeper voice than I expected. A scratched voice, the accent indefinable – Swedish? Dutch? She held out her hand. 'Max calls me Friday.'

'Because we met on one,' Max said tonelessly. 'Best day of my life.'

We exchanged pleasantries, the details of which are lost to me, though I remember that she asked if I would like a drink (I would), and I began to babble again about editors, advances, the terrible delays of publication, while all the while, over the sound of my voice, the words rolled deafeningly through my head: *whoareyou-whoareyouwhoareyou.* But when I stepped into the reception room I forgot all about my rambling chatter, forgot manners entirely, and stared open-mouthed at the floor.

There, oozing spit onto the Nepalese carpet – all four limbs akimbo and groping the air – was a baby.

We three were alone in the room: Max, *the baby,* and I. Max, whose slimmer physique now seemed to me more like evidence of some serious illness than a new fitness regime, collapsed into folds on the sofa.

'Help me,' he said.

His eyes rolled back into his head, exposing more of the whites than seemed healthy. His head followed, coming to rest on the back of the sofa. The strain on his neck made two cords stand out; I could see his breath running relay between them.

Friday returned with two drinks on a silver tray and I sprang back into action.

'Oh, how wonderful!' I cried, feigning an enthusiasm that babies have never inspired in me. 'Max – you've certainly kept this quiet. No wonder you've been AWOL. A new father. Big commitment. Big news *indeed.*' I took the drink Friday offered and, stepping carefully around the carpet, made my way to the nearest chair. Max scooped up the baby in an absent-minded way and placed it on his lap.

'It's a girl,' he said.

'Does Martin know?' This seemed rude, so I cast back for a more intimate question. 'What's her name?'

The baby's eyes were bright blue, like her mother's; she had the same milk-coloured lashes, the same fixed-pupil stare. On her arms and torso, long strands of white hair made intricate whorls and patterns. Her egg-shaped head was covered with a yellowish crust. Shiny pink skin glinted from under these patches, luminous in the Murano-glass lamplight.

'Beautiful,' I murmured.

Max started, looked up at me, then gazed around the room with a wondering air, as if the familiar surroundings of his house, the ink blue velvet sofa, the large-scale replica of the Cluny Mille-Fleurs tapestry – backdrop to so many of his best profile shots – were as surprising and unsettling to him as the infant that now rolled and unrolled itself on his lap in the imitation of a fat white grub.

At last he nodded, cleared his throat. 'Tuesday,' he said. 'Her name's Tuesday.' I smiled. 'Friday and Tuesday. Let me guess. Named after the day she was born.' This time he looked at me with the briefest flicker of his old roguish smile. 'Named after the day I – I mean, *we* – conceived her.'

The endless screaming. The indescribable nights of oozing parts and stinking skin. The darkness that turned into lightness and then into darkness again without an uninterrupted eight hours of sleep. All the while staring into a tiny dark hole of rage, trying to comprehend and soothe a mindless, unappeasable deity...

I imagine having a baby is tough at any age. But especially at *his*.

'It's a whole new way to do horror,' Max said wanly, propping himself against the door jamb as I once again dressed for the frigid outside world. 'Give my regards to Martin. Tell him I won't be sending him anything anytime soon.'

And with that I put Maximillian Crane out of my mind, or rather, I put him on hold. Just another paused acquaintance among the mounting number who had disappeared, at least for a time, into a black hole of nappies, playdates – and no more novels.

I didn't think about him for months. But I continued to think about Frida. Frida flying towards me in a white dress, blocks of ice in her hands that I realised, just before waking, were glaciers – the same glaciers that carved out the deep northern valley where Max had always lived. Frida, her white hair wriggling like the first signs of life in a corpse's chest, reaching out, wrapping around my body, pulling me closer to hers – and then *through* hers, beyond flesh and veins, into a starless sky where planets revolved and remade each other into the forms that humans found them. Frida behind me as I created, pulled stories from the fabric of time, singing in her rasping voice the same words that flew from my fingers.

Those were the nights. But during the day, I felt drained. Blocked. I was still riding the success of *To the Dust* but I needed a follow-up, and quickly. The dreaded blank page, now with the added weight of expectations.

So it was almost a relief when Max appeared once again in my inbox, almost a year to the day (I realised with some shock) from his last message. I opened it hopefully. Another invitation, another visit? Any distraction was welcome.

> **[no subject]**
> **o dont have access to email. wrtg from phone bt not mine. Alone now**
> **but both back soon. pls come pls help Max**

Not his usual style, I thought. Looks like he's gone experimental.

But because of the dreams – because of Frida – out of writerly curiosity, and a sudden chill – and not at all because I hadn't written a single word myself since last December – I put on my coat and caught the 6pm train to the valley.

Walking up the steep dark driveway, I let myself enjoy the

feeling of trepidation, that childhood fear of the unknown that we so rarely feel as adults, but that inevitably gives way to relief and a renewed sense of security. I'd tell Max off for wasting his creative juices on something as trivial as an invitation, not to mention the fright he'd given me. He'd tell me about how glad he was that this year of infancy was over, how good it felt to be writing again. We'd both laugh over a glass of his expensive Scotch as the warmth returned to my hands and feet.

But all these comforting thoughts left me as soon as Max's house rose into view.

Despite the wind, the front door was wide open. The lights were on in the foyer, the library, and kitchen. The opulent furnishings, and the blazing light, made the scene inside even more shocking – a real-estate agent's dream of a nightmare.

Max, or what was left of Max, was stretched out on the kitchen floor. A desiccated figure, spindly arms and legs splayed out on the grey flagstones, dressed in what seemed like a baggy beige tracksuit until I realised, with a sinking feeling, that this was folds of loosened skin. He was groaning. Without thinking, I pulled off my coat and threw it over his naked body. Running to the sink, I drew a glass of water which I held to his papery lips. 'Max…'

He turned his face and the water streamed down his chin, dislodging the crusts of sores from which oozed another clear liquid. His open mouth seemed all teeth and no gum; the healthy pink tissue had retreated back to its roots, leaving a startling expanse of bone over which his swollen tongue continually glided. I understood then, the kind of horrible epiphany that usually makes me reach for my notes, what it means to say someone is 'long in the tooth'; it means that they are dying.

Max groaned again, then flung out one bony arm with a forcefulness that surprised me. I turned in its direction.

Friday and Tuesday had entered the room. Or they had been there all along, watching.

Friday – or Frida – seemed much younger than I remembered, with the gangly-deer look of a girl. She radiated vitality; the room was full of it, like starlight. *Or was it Tuesday that I was looking at?* Because with a cold calmness I observed that they were the same age.

Twins.

They smiled in unison, opened their mouths in unison, and when they spoke it was with one voice – a hoarse voice full of ice and time. I understood then that they were not mother and daughter at all, or even twins, but two parts of a single creature.

My mind accepted this, as one accepts the ineffable. Natural law had ceased to exist; credulity was all I had left. But what they said – when their words finally pierced the thick terror in my brain – was the one thing I would never have imagined.

'We've written a novel.'

With a sound like the flurry of birds taking flight, they thrust a thick sheaf of paper towards me.

I looked from one to the other. Their faces were shining. Expectant. Glowing with the pure, untarnished hopefulness of youth. For a moment, all I could think about was how much I wanted to take that from them.

'Art begets art,' they sang. 'We found something that inspires us.' From the floor, Max made a sound between a whimper and a howl. 'What did you *do* to him?'

'The world doesn't need Max anymore. The world has us now.'

'The world has always had you.' I said these words before I thought them. Pulling Max to his feet, I wrapped his fleshless arm around my shoulders. He weighed no more than a bundle of firewood, but when I stepped forward, his dangling feet caught the edge of a flagstone and I stumbled.

Friday-Tuesday reached out from across the room and caught Max as he fell.

Cradling him like a child, his emaciated arms and legs nearly reaching the floor, they advanced on the kitchen island. Solid Calcutta marble, another of Max's luxuries. Idiotically, I thought: ideal for meal prep and morgues.

And then –

My memory baulks at Max's suffering, rears up and speeds away. I don't want to remember what happened next, let alone write it down for perpetuity. Why does the world need more horror, anyway?

But I have to. That's the deal. So.

Solid Calcutta marble.

Friday-Tuesday lifted Max onto the island. Side by side, each with one arm extended, they reached together into Max's mouth. Down his throat, which expanded sideways, like a fish's opening gills. Down into whatever came at the end of human pipes and tunnels.

And they...*rummaged.*

'Not much wine left in this raisin,' they said musically.

Max's eyes bulged. I would prefer to believe he was already dead at this point, but I saw live tears stream down his face.

They found whatever they were looking for, rummaging deep in Max's belly. They pulled and pulled. With one violent jerk they brought it up, up through his pipes and out of his mouth. It came out with a wet, sucking sound, while the rest of his innards, still attached, came along with it.

They'd turned Max inside out.

And set about devouring whatever they held in their hands, not neglecting the bloody flesh heaped beside their elbows.

As they ate, they glowed.

The story could end right there. I'm sure my publisher would prefer it that way.

Max's funeral took place three weeks later, an industry affair attended by publishers, editors, press, and a hundred grim-faced or weeping young women. Even in death he found a new audience, as his especially gruesome murder – unresolved, of course – made its way into every paper.

I was on the train home from the funeral when Martin called. His voice cut in and out as we rocketed across the landscape. *Such an enormous tragedy. All here in shock. Of course concerned. Your well-being. Would you…stop by?*

The version I told Martin was the one I'd constructed over the past three weeks, with just enough detail to have the ring of truth, but not enough to get me sanctioned by mental health professionals. I told him about Max's baby, his rapid decline. The gory violence of his death. And Frida.

Frida, who had melted like the frost, leaving nothing to be investigated.

'Frida.' Martin half-closed his eyes, as if reminiscing. Then he smiled. 'Yes. I know her. I was the one who introduced her to Max.'

I tried to understand. There was something significant about what he'd just said, some implication that was far from good, but my mind failed to grasp it. Instead, it seized on something smaller. A detail, not the most significant from that night – and certainly not the most horrible – but the most incomprehensibly bizarre.

'They said… Frida said she'd written a book. Do you know anything about that?'

'A book?' Martin laughed. 'Everyone has a novel in them, these days.' His nonchalance unsettled me.

'How can you joke at a time like this?'

Martin licked his lips as though preparing for a speech. 'Well.

Let me explain it. Even the *Szyvara* have dreams, sometimes. They're drainers and destroyers – not creators – but they get ideas. Have modern ambitions. Think they can rise above their station.' He shrugged. 'What's creativity anyway? Taking something from the world, and returning it in a different form – '

The implication I'd failed to grasp was taking on shape and definition. 'You…you *knew*.'

'I knew what Frida was, yes. What she *is*. She showed up at an afterparty during last year's Frankfurt fair. Not on any guest list, I might add. I saw her talking to Castor Krombach — the poor guy could barely walk by the time she was done. I recognised her at once, from old…from *very old* times.'

I could see it fully now, the thought I'd avoided. 'You did this to Max. On purpose. But we knew him…'

'I knew Max well, yes. I knew he couldn't resist her. A woman who only gets younger?' Martin smiled. 'I thought you, as a writer, would appreciate the poetic justice.'

'You think he *deserved* this?'

'I don't think in terms of crime and punishment. But since you do – think of the greater good. No more hurt young women. No fans left disappointed by their favourite author's fall from grace. More space for newer, younger writers, with newer, younger audiences.'

I thought about Max, poor old Max, inside out on his kitchen island.

'Once he'd stopped producing, Max was only a liability. You saw his behaviour first-hand. It was only a matter of time before some poor young thing…accused him. And then what? No more back catalogue, which, frankly, was all that man was good for anymore.'

Placing both palms on his desk, Martin leaned forward – far,

far forward, farther than the width of the desk would seem to allow.

'You understand, don't you? That just isn't a risk we can take for an author past his prime.'

His face was so close that I could see every pore, each one as deep as a grave.

'Inspiration comes in many forms,' he was saying. 'We're not picky as to which – as long as the results are effective. And we're not above lending a helping hand. *Nurturing* the process. Who do you think put the opium on Poe's bedside table? The heroin in Burroughs' needle…who was responsible for that? Not the wreck who couldn't even handle a gun when his wife decided to play William Tell. A gun, I might add, that appeared, fully loaded, at just the right moment to ensure a lifetime of guilt – and some of the most horrifying works of the 20th century.'

There was water in my mouth, and a roaring there, too, as if the ocean itself was pouring down my throat. I swallowed, tried to speak, but the ocean kept on flowing.

'I could go on, right up to the present day. The cocaine that kept King productive. The young girls–'

'Stop,' I screamed, 'enough.'

Finally – thankfully – Martin leaned back. 'And you,' he continued, more softly now. 'Maybe Max was just what *you* needed.'

He opened a drawer. Took out a few papers.

'A contract for what you're going to write next. I suggest you start tomorrow. The terms are good – *if* you deliver.'

With a smile that was almost kind, he pushed the contract across the table.

Reader, I signed it. For today and tomorrow and always. The terms are good, the words drip through me slowly and steadily, and I hope – I beg the muses – that it will always be this way.

ABOUT THE AUTHOR

LILY KADE has worked as a marketing copywriter for more than a decade, helping brands tell lies and contributing to the horror of late-stage capitalism. This is her first foray into fiction of the upfront kind.

GHOST HUNT

ADRIAN TCHAIKOVSKY

'Naturally,' Dr Fantod had said to him, 'when we decided to sell a limited number of these *experiences*, you were one of the first people we thought of.'

And maybe that was true and maybe it was just her buttering his ego. Max could think of a dozen people at his golf club alone who had both money and trophy collection enough to make them eligible for her pitch. Another half-dozen who put on the red of the Balesly Hunt, maybe, and certainly a full twenty at White's or Carlton's. Money, yes. Guns and a love of shooting them at all God's creatures, certainly.

Perhaps not the other thing. Because Fantod's pitch had been decidedly *odd*. What she was selling wasn't for just your average huntin' and shootin' fellow. Needed someone willing to take risks on a curious new venture. Or just someone who was really, *really* keen on bagging something special.

Maxwell FitzPattern was aware, at the back of his mind, that he was the latter more than the former. But he really *was* the latter. There was a part of his brain that just couldn't get its serotonin fix unless he'd pulled the trigger on some poor beast. And while grouse and deer and even rabbits would slake it in a pinch, he'd made sure to bag a lion while there were still lions left to bag. And tigers and bears too, oh my! As MP for a very safe Lincolnshire seat he had a firm sense of the order of the world, the hierarchy of it as confirmed to him by the vicar every Sunday. Rich man, castle; poor man, gate; man given dominance over nature. Meaning, as far as he was concerned, he was allowed to hunt, shoot, and fish it.

Fantod's operation was on former MOD land, a great stretch of cratered wilds used for war games and artillery practice up until thirty years ago, after which it had mostly sat idle or played host to scout troops. There was still a broad tarmacked track into it, better quality than the actual B-road Max had sped down, safe in the knowledge that he knew the Chief Constable. And Fantod plainly needed the access. Even as Max turned in, there were heavy goods vehicles moving out with emptied flatbeds. When he reached the car park he saw not just the Portakabins they'd thrown up for hospitality, but some kind of heavy machinery a team of engineers was bolting together.

It was already late afternoon, the September twilight creeping up on them. Fantod had explained this was a hunt best pursued after dark. As was, he supposed, traditional.

He was the last to arrive, his BMW pulled up alongside a rank of similarly expensive machines, some with chauffeurs idling beside them. He knew some of the personalised plates. A whole *Who's Who* of potting dumb animals had pitched up from all over the country.

A young man wearing a Fantod Labs hoodie approached and took him over to the lit Portakabin, where he had a brief flurry of renewing acquaintance, handshakes, and backslapping. Mostly men, mostly around his own fifty years or so, mostly good family. One fellow who was some sort of American music chappie, and another who'd done very well in selling imaginary money on the internet, but they were off to one side, beyond the pale.

He accepted a glass of bubbly just as Fantod came in, with that bright bounce she did, trying to take a decade off her age. She was small, fair, had come up out of Cambridge: physics, philosophy, theology. He supposed that was the very specific trajectory that got you into this rum sort of business.

'Ladies and gentlemen,' she announced. 'I'm not going to keep you waiting for long, but before we turn everything *on*, I think a brief introduction and explanation is warranted. The science of the business, because it *is* science we're doing here. I know some of my colleagues wanted to dress it up as something "*spooky*" but honestly I think what we've got here is more impressive without the legerdemain. Welcome, therefore, to the first ever real-life ghost hunt. Tonight, each of you is going to get the opportunity to go after game such as you never even imagined possible.'

She had a very particular grin, Doctor Sally Fantod. Bright, hard to look at, a bit deranged. Not really selling the *science* of it, but her audience was composed of people already sold on her pitch, so everyone made allowances.

'As physicists have delved into the substance of the quantum realm,' she went on, 'certain discontinuities have been discovered, from which we can deduce the existence of hitherto unknown phenomena, and by such logical deductions expand our understanding of the universe. There you go, a brief history of the last century of particle physics explained.' Another cracked grin. 'Until very recently, until my own as-yet-unpublished discoveries, some of the ways the cosmos was behaving remained very peculiar, leading to all manner of outlandish theories to account for them. Dark Energy, eh? Who really believed in that? When, of course, some of these phenomena had an explanation much closer to home, and to longstanding human experience. I am, of course, talking about ghosts.'

A few laughs, a little derision. A shuffling amongst the great and the good, people who hadn't come here to be made fools of.

'Ghosts,' Fantod repeated. 'Formed when a bioelectric system of sufficient complexity comes to an end and dissipates its pattern into the underlying fabric of space-time. And while some patterns are stronger than others – those who died with a greater agitation of neuroelectricity, say – the residual patterns of every single complex system that ever was are preserved in the matrix of the world. Sagan said we're all star stuff, right? But what we also all are – or will be – is ghosts.' And her grin widened as if this was the greatest revelation in history. Her audience stared at her, silent and somewhat stony. They had not come here to have some line of suspect pseudoscience sold to them. The unappreciated silence stretched out a little, and Fantod laughed nervously.

'One hundred thousand years ago,' she told them all, 'mammoths walked this land. Walked here all the way from mainland Europe. Walked here and died here, and their ghosts remain.'

Nobody said anything, but the calibre of the quiet changed distinctly. Max felt the hairs prick on the back of his neck. And it was nonsense, and any moment she'd be asking for more money, or this would be some Channel 4 exposé on the gullible rich. And yet *something* in him shivered.

She led them out, then. Apparently that was all the explanation they were getting. Outside, into a darkness lit by the fierce white glare of floodlights. Out to the lip of the hollow so they could look down at the Machine. A capital M seemed to be warranted.

It was a vast ring of interlocking sections, festooned with bundles and coils of wiring. A handful of laptops were connected into it, set on folding tables at what was probably a safe distance. A couple of Fantod Labs staff were crouching there, tapping away.

Fantod pitched her voice up to carry. 'Why, you ask, don't we see ghosts all the time? Why is it the province of certain places, or people, unreliable and impossible to prove? Well as to the latter, I'm about to make ghosts the solid province of the scientist, amenable to research and beyond reasonable doubt. As to the former, ghosts are just one part of the myriad universal interactions that go on beneath our notice. Only under very particular personal or environmental conditions are the strongest spectral imprints perceivable. However, as with everything, once we understood that, we were able to design apparatus to permit apprehension of the apparition.' She paused, apparently in the hope someone would find this wordplay clever. Nobody gave any indication of it. 'When this machine is activated,' she went on, 'it will produce a quantum resonance that will magnify the waveforms of the ghosts themselves. A specific vintage and quality of ghosts, from amongst the layered strata of psychic imprints pressed into the world. Make them visible to the unassisted eye in a radius of almost two kilometres.'

But she had pushed the patience of her audience too far. They shuffled, they muttered, they talked amongst themselves. Fantod waved at her technicians, foregoing any more of her speech.

Someone threw the switch. A cascade of sparks danced around the circumference of the ring, slowly at first, then faster and faster. The air fizzed with ozone. Half the floodlights popped. Someone let out a hoarse cry of fright.

The deep bass throb of the engine rose higher and higher – no, Max thought. Not higher, but... *further* somehow. The sound expanding out in a direction he'd never had cause to consider before, as though ascending to some other plane of existence. Until he could feel the vibration of it beneath his feet, but couldn't hear it at all, though simultaneously the air seemed filled with it.

And then…

Nothing. For a breath Max would have accepted anything. Choirs of angels, the face of God, ancient aliens. That moment passed without anything obvious manifesting, and he frowned about, and met others frowning back at him, and nothing seemed to have changed, except…

Something flared briefly in the dark, sparking gasps of alarm. Max was left with the afterimage of a woman in a long dress, her face turned away, receding into the dark. Then, further, he thought there was a flurrying of motion. More the suggestion of movement than anything substantial. Save that he was left with the impression of horses, riders.

For an instant he saw a block of segmented armour and rectangular shields, the flare of a phantom eagle.

'Think of it,' came Fantod's voice, 'a little like tuning a radio, eh? Ah, there we go!'

The man next to him – he was on the board of a pharma giant, Max recalled – was pointing, staring, face gone completely slack. His mouth worked but no sounds came out. Max followed the line of his pointing digit.

Off in the dark, something was moving. Something pale and lit from within by its own pallid glow. More than one, flowering into existence. Something ancient emerging into this new-minted night. Max stared for a long time before his eyes could parse what he was seeing. Distant, but the scale of them somehow communicated itself. Great, swaying things wreathed in trailing hair that drifted about them like the tresses of drowned things. Tree-trunk legs that trailed into nothing before they could touch the prosaic modern ground. Curved tusks to put the greatest of modern pachyderms to shame. As he watched, one lifted its phantom trunk to the moon and he fancied he heard a tin-tube echo of far-away trumpeting. Distanced by one kilometre and a hundred millennia.

Fantod gave them that moment to understand what they were seeing. And maybe it was flummery, and she'd seeded the whole MOD site with holographic projectors or something, but Max knew. Something in him, some sense that had evolved in humans before these beasts became extinct, was telling him. Through the hairs on his neck and the race of his heart, telling him *Real; it's real.*

Fantod clapped her hands together, and everyone jumped. Her people were coming out of the Portakabin, carrying bundles of long, familiar implements.

'What are you waiting for?' Fantod asked them. 'Grab a gun, let's go bag some mammoths!'

Some of Fantod's staff were doubling as beaters, or at least going ahead with torches so nobody broke an ankle in a rabbit hole. And were there generations of rabbit ghosts out there to be found? Max, finding himself walking alongside Fantod, asked her.

'Perhaps,' she allowed. 'But you'd see them as no more than smudges if you saw them at all. It's intellect, consciousness, that creates the complexity of waveform for a properly apprehensible spectre,' she explained, and by then they were closer still, and the scale of the things – the name no lie! – was astonishing. Greater than any living elephant. Vast, silent, insubstantial behemoths drifting like dirigibles above the bristly modern grass. Their eyes were holes onto a void that gave Max's innards a twist for a moment. Below the trunk and tusks their narrow mouths opened onto infinity. There was something terrible to them. An awful grandeur, like the spread sails of a ghost ship. He needed them to make noise; to thunder and trumpet and stomp. That would bring them into the realm of the physical, where he was the master.

'Do they know we're here?' asked a nearby vulture capitalist nervously. Max joined the majority in wrinkling his nose, snorting with disdain. Inside, he asked, *Well do they?*

'These are only afterimages,' Fantod told them. 'They are the imprint of a thinking being left on the fabric of the universe after it has died. They may seem to react to you but that's just a coincidence, some ancient recorded behaviour seeming to reflect what's happening in the here and now.' And was there a slight hollowness to her voice, right then? Did Max feel that she was glossing over nuances she didn't want to share? But the moment passed, and the pharma exec was saying, 'I mean fine, we see them,' as though spectral mammoths were, in and of themselves, no great feat. 'What are we supposed to do with them? Can't exactly stick their heads on the trophy wall, can we? What's *this* supposed to do to them?' He weighed the gun in his hands.

Fantod's smile was polite and perfect. 'The cartridges your weapons are loaded with,' she explained, 'are full of a very carefully prepared mix of silver, iron, sodium chloride and allicin. A mixture that has been found to disrupt the waveform patterns that have been made visible to you.'

The pharma exec snorted. 'And then what? They just come back tomorrow night for your next crowd of punters, I suppose.'

'Not at all. Once a particular waveform has been broken, that's it, gentlemen. Removed from the world. Each living thing creates precisely one ghost, and when – *busted*, shall I say? – then it's gone. Gone for good. Extinct.' Her grin was like a razor. 'You can't take a souvenir of your kills, no, but you can know for sure that you brought something unique to an end.'

And that, Max considered, was what counted, in big-game

hunting. Not the lion's head on the wall but the knowledge that, after all the lions were all gone, *you*'d had your part in it.

There must have been well over a hundred mammoths breezing across the dark ground out there, luminous against the blackness. More than enough to ensure no two gallant hunters would end up bagging a stockbroker or commercial landlord for the pot along with their ghostly prey. Max strode out, feeling that adrenaline spiral inside him that only this sort of pursuit brought out. To take something from the world. To demonstrate his mastery. And – just like popping a tiger at five hundred metres with the best sight and rifle money could buy – a mastery enforced by there being zero actual peril to himself. If it had been about Man Versus Wild he'd go after the blighters with a pointed stick, after all. No point giving Mother Nature a fighting chance.

And he advanced, and kept on advancing, and the mammoths, well they grew only more mammoth. Until he could stare at that vast flank of wispy, ghostly hair as though it was the side of a house. Until the soles of his feet twitched with anticipation for leaden steps he couldn't feel. He stared up at them, and thought about Fantod's 'intellect, consciousness.' That this thing was something that *thought* and *felt* enough – no, *had* thought and felt enough – to leave behind this afterimage of the creature it had been. He had to forcibly remind himself that it was, after all, just that.

He put the shotgun to his shoulder, sighted down the barrel – couldn't bally *miss*, could he? – and pulled the trigger. The gun itself kicked and roared just as he was used to, and the other mammoths, all that grand herd stretching off into mere blurs in the distant dark, did not react to the sound as a herd of real animals might. But his target! In the very centre of its great haunch he saw a fist of darkness where the scatter of shot had gone in. A darkness that grew and sucked the lambent wisps of the mammoth inwards. Like a black hole. Like water down a plug. The great breadth of the beast pouring in a hungry vortex into nothing at all. Into the night sky behind it. Into utter oblivion.

And it reared, and lifted its trunk to heaven, and he thought he heard a distant hollow echo of panicked elephantine sounds. *Ancient recorded behaviour*, he reminded himself. And in a way that was better, though in a way it was also worse, because when he shot something he wanted it to *know* it had been shot.

Only then did he become aware of the others.

They were beyond the space the mammoth had occupied, about the same distance from the vanished beast as he was. For a moment he actually thought it was some of Fantod's people, or his fellow hunters. But it wasn't. Wasn't them. Wasn't people. *Was* people, somehow. Almost.

Half a dozen of them, glimmering in the dark. Stocky, clad in cloaks and many layers of hides. Long hair bound back with beads and cords. Beard, for the men among them. Broad, flat faces, heavy brows and jaws. The eyes were dreadful. Just holes like sucking wounds, as the mammoth's had been. Bigger, compared to the visages they were set in. Hollow, hungry sockets in the glimmering smudges of their faces.

Cavemen, he thought. And they weren't all men and probably they didn't live in caves, but they were cavemen as far as he was concerned.

'What?' he demanded of them. And of course they didn't answer, and of course they couldn't see him. They were just looking towards the mammoth, which meant through the space the mammoth's ghost had occupied before he'd dispersed its waveform into the background radiation of the universe or whatever-the-hell.

'I shot your dinner, is that it?' he asked them. He was trying for mirth but their reproachful dead stare was starting to get to him. They weren't really there, and *he* wasn't there for them. It was just coincidence they were staring at him so pointedly. *Ancient recorded behaviour.*

'You'll not get anywhere in life just standing about!' he told them mockingly. 'No wonder you all went extinct!' And probably that didn't make a lot of sense, but he strongly felt that these slack-jawed troglodytes weren't anything *he*'d claim as ancestors. And still they stared. Eyelessly, impossibly, judgingly, they stared.

'Oh to hell with you,' Max said, raised the gun and let them have it with the other barrel.

The lash of the salt and metal granules caught the two in the middle, and he saw the same pattern of gnawing dark appear across the brightness of their images. They funnelled away into nothing like the mammoth had, and if their faces seemed to wear agony and grief it was only the way that their dissipation stretched and distorted them. They were just echoes. They had died a hundred thousand years ago, probably from standing around until they starved to death. *Idle sods. Not my ancestors. Probably some of my employees' though!* And he chuckled grimly at that.

He reloaded and bagged another couple of mammoths, but the novelty had worn off. A worthwhile venture, though. He wondered if dinosaurs had been complex enough to leave ghosts. Now *there* was something he could pitch to Fantod…

On the way back, something made him look over his shoulder. There they were, the remaining cavemen. Phantom Neanderthals hovering in the dark, still staring, still judging. Following. Which just meant, he thought nervously, that they'd come this way all those aeons ago, and he was coincidentally retracing their steps.

Back with Fantod and the others, and the machine still generating its ghost-conjuring field, nobody looked at the cavemen. Nobody mentioned them, as they hung there at the very edge of the light, staring cavernously at those who had come to replace them. Who had now reached back through history to make sport of the herds they had once hunted. But then Max didn't mention them either. He felt that it wouldn't show him in a good light, and that maybe someone would think he was uneasy about their continued presence. And so nobody said anything, and the cavemen might as well not have been there at all.

Fantod made a final speech. Thanks for their generous donations, reassurances she'd contact them for the next phase of the project, invitations to get in touch if anyone wanted a repeat outing. Max glanced around at his fellows and reckoned that, actually, nobody did. She'd have to find a new crop of suckers. She'd delivered exactly what she promised, but the experience had proved curiously… insubstantial.

The cavemen watched, as he handed back the gun. As he walked briskly for the cars. He hung back, in fact. Let the others rev their engines and set off. Almost asked Fantod, *Are you sure they can't see us?* Almost asked her, *How far can they follow you?* They'd turned the machine off by then, but he could still see *them.*

'Oh the field hangs about for a few hours,' Fantod said blithely, because he really *did* ask about that. And she didn't quite look at him. Nor at the cavemen. Just gave the impression of a very busy woman who had a lot of packing up to do.

The spectres watched him get into his Beemer, and he was struck by an unwanted revelation. When he hit the main road, he'd have left the radius of the machine and its field, but that didn't mean the ghosts weren't still *there*, did it? Ghosts were everywhere. The machine didn't call them into being, just made them visible. He found the thought didn't upset him as much as the idea that *these* ghosts might just follow him. However ineffective they were. No matter he'd never know or have to look at their haunted, haunting faces ever again.

Fantod was looking at him, one eyebrow crooked. Something in his body language had betrayed a weakness, let her know he'd been on the point of asking for advice. Putting himself in her power, when he was the hunter, the rich man, the one in control of things. She was just some Barnum-esque carney with a doctorate. He told himself that and it made him feel better about things.

He closed his car door and pulled away, leaving the whole weird business behind.

It was in the mirror, first. Apparently the machine's influence was sufficient to give the things reflections. Fleeting, pale forms, flickering in the rear-view. Heavyset humanoid figures, arms pumping, legs fading to nothing before they could touch the rough tarmac of the old MOD track. The determined, powerful gait of the mammoth hunters who – being dead – could run forever.

He put his foot down. For a moment his view was clear of them, then somehow they were matching him. Closing with him. Those terrible void-eaten eyes burned into his own through the silver of the mirrors.

The left front tyre was abruptly skidding from the bitten edge of the path and onto uneven ground. Max hauled at the wheel to drag the car back on course. How stupid, when these things were just wisps, just echoes, if he got *himself* killed through carelessness. And really, he should slow down. What did it matter if they caught up? If they occupied the other seats of the car, insubstantial feet pounding away like a family of Flintstones? But somehow he didn't want that. Didn't want them there. Put his foot down further, kept his eyes to the road.

When he next caught the flicker it was in the corner of his eye. He couldn't help but look. There was a caveman running there, keeping pace even though he was doing fifty-five, which was twenty more than the track really allowed. For a second Max couldn't tear his gaze from the apparition. That barrel-bodied form somehow pelting along, matching his reckless speed. Phantom hair blowing into nothing as its head turned, those eyes, those hungry, accusing eyes!

He looked forwards and there was someone on the road, right before him. For a moment his instincts kicked in; stamping for the brake, wrestling with the wheel, about to careen right off the track and probably into an uncleared minefield or something. Then he registered it was just another caveman. One more ghost, desperately standing in the way of progress. A spear drawn back to throw, even. In that moment something flipped in his mind. They weren't frightening at all. They were desperate and sad, and contemptible. And *he* was important. *He* was the hunter here, and they were just prey.

He rammed his foot onto the accelerator, hunched over the wheel, and ran the caveman down.

Ran through it, of course. His car wasn't made of the weird holy water compound Fantod had loaded the guns with. The vehicle and the spectral caveman momentarily occupied the same space, and he flinched from some terrible chilling touch, the bite of the grave, *something*. But there was nothing. The fringes of the ghost passed through his body, yet touched him not at all.

He put a foot on the brake at last, a long skid to a halt. Looking in the mirror at the spectre left behind him. It had turned, and he could just make out the hollows of its eyes. Dejected, he thought, at its lack of leverage on the world.

He chuckled. Suddenly he was feeling far better about himself.

He opened the car door and slid out, looking back at the hapless creature.

'You're dead!' he shouted at it. 'We out-evolved you! We're better than you! You're all dead and we're still here!'

There was another flicker of movement, and he turned to see a new caveman on the road, just a few feet away. Standing there, staring because staring was all they had. Impotent, like the rest.

'What?' Max jeered at it. 'Come to complain? Kill your dinner and your friends and mess up your site of special scientific interest? Nobody cares, mate. You're the past and nobody cares!'

The thunderous trumpeting sound rattled every bone in his body, and for a brief moment Max regretted every moment because the mammoths had come. The mammoth herd was charging, surely. He could feel the shake of the ground and his ears rang to their furious cry. In the next instant his modern mind recontextualised the sound: not some prehistoric beast but a truck. One with Fantod Labs livery on it, come to take away the pieces of her machine. Honking its horn, because the driver saw a stopped car on the other side of the street, because the driver saw…

The caveman, in the truck's path, turned sanguine into its blazing headlamps and held out its arms. Bright against the darkness, as the last revolutions of the machine drew its spectral image from the depths of time. Max saw the driver, high up in the cab. Saw his face, the whites of his wide, panicked eyes. Saw him fight the wheel to avoid this sudden pedestrian in his way. The whole great flat hammerhead of the truck radiator grill twisting towards his stopped car. Towards *him*.

After, he could at least pick himself up. Hear the hiss of water and the horrified gasping of the driver. The creaks of crumpled bodywork. Formerly his BMW, now rolled under the front wheels of the truck. And, also under the wheels, him. The rest of him. The meat of him. The mess that formerly had been him.

He opened his mouth. No sound came. Nothing. He took a shaky step and felt no contact with the ground.

Across from him, the cavemen stared. Empty eyed, shadowy. Yet somehow more substantial than they had been. Or perhaps it was relative. Perhaps it was that his own *substance* had gone under the wheels.

One of them took a step forwards. There was a spear in its hand. The head was flint and Max could see, with the holes of his own eyes, the intricate contours of its sharp, sharp edges.

The caveman grinned with big, square teeth, behind which there was only hungry nothing.

Max backed away. He turned, he fled.

Behind him, unhurried, filled with grim anticipation, the hunters followed.

ABOUT THE AUTHOR

ADRIAN TCHAIKOVSKY was born in Lincolnshire and studied zoology and psychology at Reading before becoming a professional author in 2007. He is a keen role-player and board gamer and is trained in stage-fighting. His literary influences include Gene Wolfe, Mervyn Peake, China Miéville, Steven Erikson, Naomi Novak, Scott Lynch, and Alan Campbell.

Adrian primarily explores deep themes, such as artificial intelligence and alien awareness within epic galactic and fantastical settings. He has a deep interest in the animal world, specifically insects from his studies in Zoology, and has a particular penchant for spiders.

His awards include: BSFA, Audible, Galaxy Awards, Neffy, Golden Dragon, Sidewise Awards, Arthur C. Clarke, and BFA.

THE MIDNIGHT BURN

TL HUCHU

Contrary to what the tabloids may claim, the most triumphant thing a migrant may do is to go home having served their time in hell. It's not that the First World is wholly without charm; certain amenities like reliable electricity, or cheap, unlimited Wi-Fi, and maybe even freedom of speech have their appeal, but for Tapuwa Mambuza the sheen had long ago worn off. The greys in his hair and stubble matched his weatherbeaten face which fitted like a wrinkly coat, shrunk at the back of the wardrobe after the moths had their way with it. He had dark rings round his eyes, heavy bags below. All he wanted was to go back home.

A baby was crying in the next room. It couldn't have been from Tapuwa's flat, his missus had left with their three children a while back. It must the neighbour's child. His wife, his children. Gone.

Tapuwa's knees creaked when he got out of bed. His calves ached. It took a while for his limbs to wake up. He had to stretch a bit before he could get going. It made him feel the weight of each minute, because he pictured himself young, ambitious, hungry, fresh off the boat not so long ago. At forty-eight, he could only wonder where the time had gone. Three decades passed in the blink of an eye as he looked outside the window of his flat on the eleventh floor of a tower block. It was gloomy and grey outside. In the harsh midwinter there was no real difference between day and night, both marked by the incessant tick of the clock. Hanging in the fog, small yellow circles, streetlights battling the press of darkness. It was the colour of gold turned to rust.

It was before three in the morning and his bladder was screaming. He could no longer do the entire night before needing to spend a penny; twice, sometimes more times than he could count, enough to round up to a pound. The flat was cold, as was the bare blue carpet beneath his toes. Only the bed in which Cynthia was softly snoring was warm and inviting. She was young, and when she slept it was hard to rouse her. Tapuwa fought the urge to wake her up for a chat, instead covering her bare shoulder with the duvet and walking out of the bedroom into the corridor, avoiding switching on the light, which would be too bright. He was about to burst.

After he relieved himself, he went to the living room and stood by the window. It didn't bring relief because even afterwards he felt full, like he was about to explode. Six months since he moved in, he'd not yet gotten round to buying new curtains. There was a two-seater sofa against the wall, and the twenty-inch TV sat on a solitary wooden dinning chair. What need did he have for furniture here anymore? Tapuwa had unburdened himself of the material things that had seen him come to this land of plenty. In those years he had accumulated a decent potbelly which he rubbed, gazing outside at the bone man whose stall in the square was trading during the witching hour. The seconds ticking off loudly came from the boiler timer in the kitchen next door.

Tapuwa waited, listening, making sure Cynthia wasn't up

before he went to his hidden stash. He raised one corner of the carpet on the left side of the room, near the TV, revealing a broken floorboard. There was a loud knock on the door, which made him jump. His heart thumped and he replaced the carpet back in its place, running his hand over it to make sure it took. He was filled with a dread as the door was banged on again. He covered his mouth with his hands and shrank back into the wall.

Cynthia woke up, he could hear her moving on the bed.

The banging intensified with greater urgency and Tapuwa squeezed his eyes shut. It was a horrible sound, not so much a knock, but more like someone desperately trying to break the door down. His breath escaping through covered lips was hazy, wisps, like cigarette smoke.

Cynthia came into the room, naked except for beads around her waist, her body perfect in the light pouring in from outside. Her afro was puffy and well-kempt though she'd just risen. She had big eyes and a small button nose like it was drawn in by a lazy animator. Everything about Cynthia was perky as her personality and she flashed him a smile, pearly white teeth showing. She had her phone in one hand. Always on social media, scrolling video after video.

'What are you doing?' she asked.

'Junkies. This estate is filled with them. I hope they didn't startle you?' he whispered, and it came out more as a hiss.

'I've got the munchies, you better not have had my caramel Biscoff ice cream,' she answered.

'Don't make so much noise. They'll hear.'

'Why don't you call the police?'

'No! No police… Get your ice cream if it will keep you quiet,' he whispered angrily.

'You know I don't like it when you leave me alone like this. I get nightmares.'

Cynthia yawned and turned for the kitchen. She rummaged through the fridge as Tapuwa tried to calm himself. The strain was getting to him. It's always hardest before you ascend to the next stage in life, he thought to himself. One more night and he'd be gone from this estate, this shit. That wasn't long at all. He just had to keep his shit together. Thirty years of hard work shouldn't be undone by junkies nor Tories. He got up, limbs trembling, and moved from the floor to the sofa.

He looked back at the corner of the room to make sure everything was back in place. Cynthia was his girl now, but it was too soon for her to know his secrets. A man must play his cards near his chest, especially if he was holding a good hand. He was the leader and she had to follow. If you've once made the mistake of marrying a strong personality, the sort of woman who always got her way, you weren't keen to do so again. But that problem was solved now. Tapuwa was moving on with his life – he was no simp, not anymore.

'Tea, coffee?' Cynthia asked. 'The bone man's collecting again tonight.'

'Tea.'

'Earl Grey or Yorkshire or herbal instead?'

'Any, please. Damn it!'

'What you getting mad at me for?'

'I'm sorry.'

'I wonder how many fingers and toes he'll have bought by the end of the night. I heard for a digit the bone man will give you the most beautiful flower you've ever seen. He collects them from a secret cave near the summit of Ben Nevis. No one's ever been able to find it. The flower has petals that fill your house with love and warmth, and if you chew the stem, you see the loved ones you lost. It blossoms an hour after you buy it and rots by the morning.'

Tapuwa had heard stories of the bone man that floated around the estate. He was sure the urban legend was a cautionary tale about the drug dealers in the area whose poison ruined lives. This housing estate had once been a thriving working class locale, mod cons and all, before heroin and Thatcher hit it with a double whammy. He'd not been there to see the damage, and a huge chunk of his stay in this city had been in upscale Somerton, but he'd known the aftershocks of the neoliberal earthquake hadn't seen much rebuilt around this part of town. No, Tapuwa wasn't a part of this. The neighbours, too many of them unemployed, shuffled about like flies caught in honey, clueless of the fact they'd hit the jackpot. This country's sweetness was what did them in. Unlike the natives, he was a man who came with a dream to make money, build a nice house back home and leave before the casino beat him. You had to be smart about the immigration thing. Plan. Execute. Escape.

'Baby, do you love me?' Cynthia asked, handing him a hot mug.

'Sit down and eat your ice cream. It's rude to eat while you're standing,' Tapuwa replied.

'You can be such an old dafty, you know? Luckily, I love you just the way you are.' She popped a spoonful of ice cream in her mouth and smacked her lips.

I bought that, Tapuwa thought. Fuck what anyone else says about this world; in the final analysis, the only thing that matters is the coin in your wallet. Tapuwa was too old and world weary to believe in love anymore. He sipped on his herbal tea and wished Cynthia was still in bed so he could think. A man needed time to think to himself, to plan. The tea tasted bitter, somewhat sharp but with layers to it. There were notes hidden in it, a sharp tang that you didn't get from any café or supermarket stuff. It was mixed in with an earthiness, which maybe explained that fungal hint of flavour.

'How do you make this?' he asked.

'That's my secret,' she replied with a laugh, and she blew him a kiss.

Yeah, she was into him. Don't give her too much of yourself, he thought. Keep an element of mystery. He'd got this off some guy on YouTube; an old dog like him who used to be super romantic could still learn a new trick or two. Tapuwa would stay sharp, alert, at the top of his game. He was nearly home. Sunshine and freedom awaited. He'd bought the air tickets already, business class on Qatar Airlines. It would be his first time flying business – well worth the wait. Thinking about it all made him anxious. He played around with his ring finger, empty now, the faint line blended in with his dark skin.

'Can you smell that smoke?' Tapuwa asked.

'I can't smell anything,' she replied.

'It's really strong.'

'There's nothing there. Why are you so paranoid?'

It was lodged deep inside his nostrils, wood, plastic, flesh, like someone was having a barbecue and put the kids' toys in the grill. Tapuwa remembered the Grenfell Towers in London, how many innocent people had burnt to death. They blamed it on the cladding. He didn't much like being in a high-rise, but his circumstances dictated as much.

'Did your ex-wife have to put up with this paranoia?' Cynthia asked, teasing.

'Don't talk about her. What's wrong with you? I need to take a walk and clear my head,' he said, jumping up. His ears were ringing. 'She didn't love me the way you do. You're mine.'

'Baby, it's dark outside. Don't leave me alone. Let me feed you.' Cynthia was a feeder, though her own shape didn't show it. She was lean, almost bony. Her shoulders poked out of her dress.

'I'll be back soon. You're safe here,' Tapuwa said, jumping up. His heart was thumping through his ribcage and he clutched his chest.

Was he having a heart attack? This happened to men his age. No. It happened to other people. He made sure he ate right and walked ten thousand steps a day. Yeah, he wasn't a beefcake anymore and his hairline was gone, but he wasn't the worst middle-aged man out there. Tapuwa staggered out. His legs still hadn't quite woken up. There was a strange sensation underneath his feet, a numbness, and he was stomping around so he could sense where he was in space.

'I'm afraid,' Cynthia moaned.

'Of what?' he asked, harsh and annoyed.

'Ghosts. I hear them every night. You know it's true. Zvipoko are there and something feels very wrong about this place. Please don't leave me alone here.'

'You listen to too many folk tales. Be rational, woman.'

'I told you I was marked by the people from my village back home. The spirits are after me, Tapuwa. They wanted me to be a n'anga, a spirit medium, channelling messages between the ancestors and the living, but I fled for Europe. Look at what they did to me.'

You wouldn't notice it unless you knew, but Cynthia had nyora, two tiny scars between her eyebrows, made by a razor blade when her family had taken her to the n'anga to be inducted as a medium. She'd escaped and sought asylum in Europe where such beliefs had long since faded into the stuff of fantasy fiction and history tours. Tapuwa did notice she maintained her superstitions: would never pass you salt hand to hand, spilt a drop to the ancestors when she drank, and she spoke back to the wind sometimes, using a language unknown to anyone but herself. She saw spirits lurking in the corners of buildings and said she felt cold if she walked over someone's unmarked grave. When the woodwork in the flat creaked at night, Tapuwa found himself getting scared by it as if she was infecting his psyche. He needed to be careful. Some of these little behaviours annoyed him, but this was also what he wanted. A woman who was a bit broken, who had fled and would look to him for protection. She was a woman he could control, and her traditional values meant he always got the final word, unlike with his ex-wife, who was a mistake. He'd married that one because of pressure from his people after she got knocked up. It had been a rocky marriage, she was domineering, an alpha, and he'd felt like he was a child, not her husband. He saw in Cynthia something damaged, a woman scared of her own shadow – she would always need him. He could always control her.

Tapuwa left her in the living room. A man must never explain too much to his woman. Once his decision is made, that is that, sadza rekuboarding. He looked through the peephole and made sure the coast was clear before unlocking the door and pocketing the key. Leave it open just in case.

The lift was too narrow, so Tapuwa took the stairs instead. The lighting was dim, some of the fixtures were bust, and a box of KFC lay overturned on the eighth floor, bones strewn across the steps to the landing below. Cigarette ash. The cleaners came in once a week, not nearly enough to take care of this. He made his way down as quick as he could, hurrying because another set of footsteps was following close behind.

'Cynthia, is that you?' His voice echoed in the stairwell, but no one answered. A laugh. No, he'd imagined that. There was no one coming down, but he still felt relieved opening the secure steel door below and rushing outside. He took a deep breath and let the foggy air enter his lungs. Gasped like a fish; the cold was even harsher outside. There was a hint of pale light, the moon smothered behind grey clouds.

The bone man was on one side of the corner, entertaining a group of teenagers in hoodies. Fragments of their voices carried through like shards of glass in the Baltic air. There was a kiddies' playground in the centre of the square and the swing went back and forth like someone was in it. Tapuwa skirted through the alleyway leading him to the back of the shops that ran perpendicular to his block of flats. It was a narrow access lane. There was a van at the back and a deliveryman had the rear open, readying papers for the newsagents on the square.

'What's the headline today?' Tapuwa asked.

'The usual doom and gloom,' the van man answered with an Indian accent.

'Nothing about me then?'

'You should be so lucky.'

The van man laughed and got on with his work. It was a hard gig, this one. Tapuwa used to have a route, back when he didn't have papers and needed to work cash in hand. His route took him out into the villages of Bornmall and Wishetting, the industrial estates on Poghamton, and he skirted the bypass all the way to the services at Asham-by-Tee. Not that he missed it, but it was a good gig. He'd listen to Capital or Forth One, pop songs that were brilliant earworms. It was all so much simpler then, he thought, going up the mound that led across Sidwell Lane and onto the footpath by the Ingram burn which ran all the way to the Tee. The blocks of flats on this part of the estate were four-storey identical buildings with pebbledash that added to the bleakness of the atmosphere. The coating peeled in places revealing brickwork underneath. There was a good bit of graffiti by local kids who'd never be Banksys or Basquiats.

A vial cracked underfoot and Tapuwa flinched. He dug into his pockets and retrieved a pack of B&H, lighting one swiftly. He'd tried vaping but it wasn't for him – the flavours were a bit too outrageous, and he liked seeing the flame glow up as he took a drag. The cigarette helped with the burning smell that was stuck in his nose hairs.

The burn gurgled as the waters ran over rock, faint white foam standing out even in the darkness.

'I'm nearly there now. Once the money is here, I'm gone, gone, gone,' Tapuwa told the night, and then he started laughing. Laughed so hard he caught a fit and tears ran down his cheeks. He felt elated. Another night and he'd cash out of the casino and leave before the pit boss took too much notice.

A woman in white was watching him from the bank beyond the burn. She was in a nightdress and there were three smaller beings next to her, like Snow White's dwarfs in descending order. The cigarette hung off Tapuwa's lip and he felt a chill deep inside his lungs as if winter had blown into his very soul. The woman was watching him, a black face, black eyes, an absence. He was seeing charring, that scent of overcooked meat in his nose. Tapuwa staggered and fell onto his knees.

'No,' he cried in anguish.

Something, a gust of wind maybe, something hard knocked him into the burn and he fell face first with a splash. It was a small stream, hardly enough water to reach the ankles. The water was ice cold; it pricked his skin like fire. Tapuwa tried to push up but a weight was set atop him. He flailed, heart pumping, desperate to break free and come up for air, but he couldn't. It was like a heavy person was sat on his back. He kicked his legs and thrashed about, panicked, desperate to come up for air. Then he opened his mouth and took a breath, the bubbling waters of the burn filled him up like thick black smoke, choking him. The pain in his lungs was unbearable. The woman and the three… children – they were watching him. He could sense it. His lungs were on fire, his entire being screaming out.

An eternity under the water.

A baptism.

Drowning was like fire.

Just as Tapuwa was fading, he felt a strong pair of hands reach down and pull him out of the burn. An angel. Everything was a blur and he was limp as he was dragged onto the bank. He tried to breathe but his lungs were full of water. Someone was saying something. Tapuwa coughed and a cup of brown water came out of his mouth. It was brutal. He coughed and spluttered, expelling water, and his first breath was not a relief, more a dagger through his chest. Air was sweet.

'That's it, breathe. Just breathe,' Cynthia said, as she cradled him.

'Ah, I, ma—'

'Breathe.'

Across from the bank the three figures watched, silent.

'They did it?' He pointed.

'Who?' Cynthia asked.

'My wife. She's trying to… Ngozi.'

'Ngozi is an avenging spirit, Tapuwa. It only happens when it has just cause. Tell me, what did you do?'

'Nothing.'

As he answered, the cool night air began to thicken and darken, going from crisp to smoky in an instant. Tapuwa shuddered as it hit him. He began to weep. He'd been carrying this for too long. It wasn't his fault… He was just trying to… It wasn't his fault. But the weight of it was too much. When he looked into Cynthia's brown eyes, it was as though she could see through him. He couldn't carry this on his own. She'd saved him, maybe she could shoulder the load with him.

'If you had been a medium, you might have been able to help me,' he said.

'I can't help if you don't tell me what is going on,' she replied. 'There are rituals that can help get rid of whatever ails you.'

'This cold burns my skin.' He was shivering.

In the distance was the sound of a car slowly driving around the estate. The three figures in the darkness watched him, judging him with their charred-out eyes. The smallest one reached out its little hand towards Tapuwa and he burst into tears.

'I didn't mean for it to happen. All I wanted was a better life for them, for me.' He was rambling and Cynthia held his hand. 'I didn't know they'd be around. My wife took the kids and went to her sister's in Milton Keynes for the weekend. I'd planned it perfectly. We had a little chippy and our flat was above it. I thought if I could cash in on the insurance, we could go home. The shop was in a good area, but I couldn't sell it. Planning was a pain. But, with a little fire we could unlock the money and go back home. I read up on it online. It's not that hard to get a little gas fire going. I'm not a bad person, please believe me.'

'I do,' Cynthia said gently.

'I went to the club, made sure cameras caught me in town. Then I went back to the chippy. I didn't know my wife had had a fight with her sister and so she came back early. They were sleeping. How could I have known? She didn't message me. Probably meant to surprise me or something. I honestly didn't know. My children.'

Tapuwa was a wreck, weeping violently, tears and mucus streaming down his face. A dam breeching, flooding the plain below. It was a release to tell the whole truth at last. He'd been acting, the grieving widower, photographs of him sombre in *The Sun* and *Daily Mail.* The man who'd lost his family in a tragic accident. A GoFundMe was set up and raised a fair bit of money to help with the funerals. A community devastated, coming together to help him.

'I couldn't bear the sympathy everyone gave me,' Tapuwa said. 'People were so nice, you know. They wanted to help me out, but I was the one who lit the match. They felt sorry for me.'

Cynthia let go of Tapuwa and stood up, taking the phone from her pocket. She looked at the screen, glowing bright in the darkness, and she checked they were live on a popular social media site. She looked across the water to where the ghosts of his family stood and she waved the phone at them.

'What are you doing? Can you see them too?' he asked, teeth chattering.

'The best lies are the ones which contain a hint of truth, Tapuwa. I am a n'anga, a spirit medium, and your wife's restless soul came to me seeking vengeance. She doesn't want you to die, but she wants you to suffer in this lifetime. Your confession has been streaming live on my socials.'

'You gave me the bone man's flower! It was in my tea and it made me…'

Tapuwa was stunned as she stepped away from him. The confusion was written all over his face – this woman who'd stepped into his life so nimbly as if to fill a void. In that moment, his terror gave way to relief. He saw his dead family still watching as he understood at last that he would not be going back home, but he would at least go to the place he truly belonged: prison.

ABOUT THE AUTHOR

TL HUCHU is the author of the *Edinburgh Nights* series, an original and gripping fantasy series for a crossover audience, published by Tor UK and Tor US. Book one, *The Library of the Dead* won the 2022 Nommo award for best novel, presented by the African Speculative Fiction society. Book two, *Our Lady of Mysterious Ailments*, published in 2022, was the winner of the 2023 Hurston, Wright Legacy Award. Books three and four in the series, *The Mystery at Dunvegan Castle* and *The Legacy of Arniston House* were published in 2023 and 2024 respectively, with the fifth and final novel in the series, *Secrets of the First School,* to come in 2025. Books one to three have been optioned by Sony Pictures, who intend to produce a TV series based on the novels.

Originally from Zimbabwe and a long-term resident of Edinburgh, Tendai is the author of two previous novels: *The Hairdresser of Harare* and *The Maestro, The Magistrate and the Mathematician*. These were published worldwide and translated into multiple languages. He has also written award-winning short fiction, with stories appearing in the Manchester Review, Interzone, AfroSF, Ellery Queen and others.

THE BUTCHER OF PUCKLEY VILLAGE

V CASTRO

Gather round
Gather round
The butcher is on the hunt
He wants a leg
He wants a finger
He wants a nut
No one is safe
No place to hide
The butcher must fill his carriage
And you are next for a ride

Callum couldn't prevent himself from laughing after saying these words into the phone.

'Stop!' said Maisy. 'Now we have to do it all over again.'

He gave her a disgruntled look. 'Alright, chill.'

'It's serious, because to get monetized on TikTok and YouTube requires a lot of work. I don't have the following I do because I put out shit content.'

He rolled his eyes. 'True. Your show is a big hit.'

'Exactly. Do you think I like staying in that shit B&B? I have big ideas for the show.'

'At least we're not camping,' he added.

'We can do the voice-over later. Let's head to the forest before dark,' said Maisy.

Callum locked the doors to his small Fiat and glanced around. 'Not as exciting as the church with those cool headstones. But saying that, it looked like any old village church across this country. The quaint farm shop, the little Spar with the one post office.... I don't get it.'

'It's all about atmosphere and how you tell the story.' Maisy took photos of the parking area. There was no one else there which was perfect. She hated her videos getting ruined by some cyclist or dog walker.

She walked from the dirt parking lot, only large enough for a few cars, towards the path that led into the trees. To their right was another small dirt road that separated the wood from a fenced field. This time of year it was usually dark by 6pm. It was nearly 5pm. Dark enough to look scary in the editing but not so dark she couldn't see where they were going.

Callum followed behind as she took a short video of the path leading into the woods then scanned the trees with her phone. When she finished, she turned to Callum. 'We'll just go far enough so I have enough video of the woods to do your voice-over, then me starting to tell the story of the village and the butcher.'

'Good. I think the pub next to the B&B shouldn't be too bad. Honestly, all the hype around these haunted places is just that. I haven't felt anything anywhere.'

She kept her eyes on the trees that had most of their leaves stripped from their branches. Their boots squelched on the muddy path.

'Maybe, but this village has a lot of stories.'

'Like that stupid rhyme.'

'And that's why we're here. You know where it comes from? A long time ago, well before both wars, there was a horrible spring and summer. There wasn't enough food for livestock or humans. Some deranged butcher got a taste for flesh and people started to go missing. One of those was a family man. His wife went to look for him at the place he usually liked to chop firewood. There was no sign of him except a bloody trail that she followed. There she found him being eaten over a fire, here, in these very woods. The butcher attacked, but in her rage she managed to kill him with his own knives. Or thought she had. After going for help the village found him trying to escape. They tied his body to a spike like a scarecrow and let the animals feast on him. He wasn't worthy of being buried in the churchyard...the very church we visited today.'

'So what? He haunts this place?'

'Who knows?' she said with a smile. 'But it's a good story.'

They stopped at a clearing strewn with cigarette butts, old Monster cans, an empty plastic litre bottle of Strongbow, and various other bits of rubbish.

'Well, it hasn't scared everyone away,' Callum said observing the debris around them.

'No. Alright. Let's take another video.'

Callum made the zipped lip hand gesture then put his hands in his pockets. He stepped back as Maisy began to film and walked by himself around the clearing. A crow landed nearby. It pecked at the ground then looked up and noticed him. He in turn glanced back at it. 'Hello, Mr Crow,' he said. Hearing his voice, it began walking towards him, pecking slowly at the ground as it came. He turned towards it, walking backwards, amused as it followed him. Then in an instant it dashed into the air, flying straight towards him. 'The fuck, dude!'

Its wings flapped in his face as it squawked and pecked at him. He covered his eyes with his hands, tried to fight it off. Tried to run away, back to Maisy.

The crow flew off through the trees and towards the field next to the wood.

He reached Maisy, shaking, watching it fly away.

'That was seriously fucked up.'

'Did that bird just attack you?'

'Yeah. Went for my eyes.' He took a deep breath, steadied himself. Tried not to dwell on it. 'Are you done yet?'

She glanced around and looked at the sky. It was getting darker, thick cloud covering what remained of the daylight. 'Yeah. I don't want to be out much longer. Plus, I want to film the B&B too.'

They began to walk back to the car when the gate on the fence separating the field and path slammed open then shut again. The noise coming out of the gloom startled them. They looked at each other.

'Maybe a fox ran through the bottom?'

Callum tried to keep his cool. 'Of course, look at that damn crow.'

They picked up the pace to get back to the car, but before they could reach it Maisy put her hand on Callum's arm; stopped walking. 'D'you hear that?'

He stopped too, listening.

Somewhere nearby the turning of rusting wheels could be heard.

'Like an old butcher's cart,' he said, trying to raise a smile. 'Laden down with dead bodies…'

Maisy took out her phone, pointed it in the direction of the sound and started filming. Neither moved. But no further sound was heard.

'C'mon, let's get to the car,' said Maisy putting her phone away.

As Callum drove out of the car park, she kept her eyes on the wood. She saw nothing but the encroaching darkness of night.

When they got inside the pub she looked at the cover of the menu. 'The Cart and Hare.' She thought of the butcher story and the sound of turning wheels they had just heard. She tried to dismiss it and turned her attention to ordering a drink.

'I'll go to the bar. What do you want?' asked Callum.

'Just a pinot grigio. You can't really go wrong with that.'

Callum walked to the bar and Maisy looked at the old photos on the wall. Above the bar was a giant wheel, like one taken from a cart. The wood was old and stained. She thought of the noise in the woods again. Shuddered.

Callum came back to the table, buzzing with excitement. 'You won't believe this. You should totally film in here too. See that wheel over the bar? It's from the butcher's cart! That photo next to it ... look.'

She glanced at the photo. It was of the church and the priest with others she assumed were villagers. Behind them was a cart. Their faces appeared stern as they stared straight at the camera.

'Yeah, the story goes that the entire village came out to watch the butcher get strung up.' Maisy took a sip of her wine. It wasn't bad for a pub in the middle of nowhere with only a tiny Co-op for a grocery store.

'The bartender said the priest burned the cart but kept this one wheel as a reminder to the evil of mankind.'

'Wow. That's interesting. And he just offered up that information?' She glanced past Callum to the bartender who looked like he was in his seventies. He stared back at her, angrily. 'Doesn't look like he did.'

'No...well I asked if there were any other places of interest to check out when it came to the butcher.'

She glanced back at the bartender who was wiping down the counter, avoiding her eye. Maisy stood up from her seat. 'I'll be right back.' She walked to the bar. 'Excuse me. You were just talking to my friend about the cart and the history of the village...the butcher.'

He stopped wiping, pulled himself up straight. Studied her before deciding to speak. 'Yes, I shouldn't have spoken of that.'

'Why not?'

'Because some things are too horrible to be spoken of. They should be left alone to die. Evil is always looking for a way to revive itself.'

'My name's Maisy. I tell real life spooky stories on YouTube and TikTok. Could I interview you?'

'Why? So more people can know about him?' he snapped back in a gruff voice.

'Yes.' She gave him a soft smile thinking he would agree. It usually worked.

His eyes grew large. 'You didn't listen, did you? I said no. He can't be called upon.'

'Why not?'

'Because the more people interested in him, the greater the risk.'

She looked puzzled. 'Risk of what?'

'That he comes back.'

Maisy almost laughed. But the old man clearly wasn't joking. Despite her feeling like there was no way he could really believe that.

'Well I haven't heard of any strange deaths around here, and I know about him,' said Maisy. 'Surely other people do as well.'

The old man seemed to realise she wasn't going to go away until he'd spoken to her. He put his bar towel down, looked directly at her. 'There's a certain way of calling him. That way's the only way to bring him back.'

Maisy was excited now. 'What is it?'

'I'm not going to tell you, am I? The few of us who know are dying of old age and when we die, it'll die with us.'

'So you won't tell me?'

'No. And I suggest you stop looking for him.' That seemed to be the end of it, but the bartender remained where he was, still curious. 'What have you uncovered so far?'

'Nothing. I'm just here to tell the story.'

'And that's all?' He looked relieved.

'Yeah. We went to the woods near the church and filmed. Nothing happened.'

'Nothing?' The relief was building on the old man's face.

'Yes, nothing.' Maisy thought. 'Well, there were a couple of things. Callum – that's him over there – was attacked by a crow.'

The old man's face drained of colour.

'And we heard a noise when we were leaving. Like an old cart-wheel slowly turning.' She smiled. 'Pretty spooky, though. Just hope I managed to film it.'

The bartender stared at her. 'Where was this?'

'The woods near the church. Where we were filming.'

'And what did you do? What did you do?' His voice was raised but not in anger, more in fear.

'Nothing, like I said.'

'Nothing?'

'Nothing. We were just filming the story. I told some of the story, Callum said the rhyme, that was it.'

The bartender staggered back, a look of pure terror on his face. 'Why would you do that? There? Why would you do that there?'

'Because it doesn't matter. It's just a kids' rhyme, that's all. Part of the story.'

'A kids' rhyme? That's what you think? That's really what you think? It's not. It's not, it's...' He leaned over the bar, looking like he wanted to grab hold of her, shake her. 'Don't go back there again and don't tell this story.'

Maisy was taken aback by his sudden outburst. She hoped Callum was recording. This was great footage. Exactly what she wanted.

'Promise me!' he said between gritted teeth. He looked like death with his translucent skin dotted with age spots. His dentures looked horrific.

'I promise,' she said, knowing she would anyway.

Maisy lay in bed tossing and turning. Unable to sleep. The sound of dripping water from the bathroom sink was incessant, insistent. She told herself it was because of that.

Frustrated, she threw off the covers and, not bothering to put on the bathroom light, entered the room intending to wrap a towel around the tap. As she grabbed the towel she glanced towards the mirror. And screamed. Looming towards her from out of the shadows was a man, hideous-looking, wearing a bloody leather apron and holding a cleaver in one hand. What appeared to be intestines hung over both his shoulders. Strings of viscera and blood dribbled down his bare chest. The loose skin around his neck and face made him look like a human turkey. His eyes were pure black. Empty, as if pecked out by a crow. And his smile … his smile … directly at her.

'I love the breasts, but the thighs are even better,' he hissed. His teeth had the shape and size of that of a horse. Her heart hammered, threatened to burst from her chest as he kept staring at her, grinning that horrific grin …

She flipped on the light.

There was nothing there. Just her own terrified reflection staring back at her.

She stood there, panting, trying to get her heart rate back to normal, telling herself it was just a dream dragged through from sleep to waking, a nightmare brought on by the day's events, her overactive imagination and too many white wines.

But she jumped when she heard something heavy fall in the bedroom. She rushed in and saw the kettle lying on the floor, water seeping into the carpet like blood oozing from a head injury. That settled it. She didn't want to stay alone for the rest of the night.

Grabbing her keys, she left, making for Callum's room. She knocked on the door, quietly, so she wouldn't wake any other sleepers on their landing, but insistent enough that he would hear her. And answer.

But there was no answer.

She put her ear to the door to see if she could hear him snoring. No sound.

She knocked harder. This time the door opened of its own accord. Not wanting to stay outside in the hall but fearful of what might lie before her, she carefully took a few steps inside the dark room. She could just make out something on the floor at the end of her bed.

A foot? Feet?

'Callum?'

She flipped on the light and screamed in horror. Her blood ran cold.

The room was like an abattoir. A butcher's abattoir. Callum lay on the bed split wide open, entrails and intestines pulled from him and strung about, adorning the room like Christmas decorations. His other internal organs lay on the bed and his eyes had been plucked out. On the wall above him written in what had to be blood was the rhyme she had made him say:

Gather round
Gather round
The butcher is on the hunt
He wants a leg
He wants a finger
He wants a nut
No one is safe
No place to hide
The butcher must fill his carriage
And you are next for a ride

The sheer white curtain, blood-stained and splattered now, blew in the breeze from the open window. Her entire body trembled.

Help. She must call for help. Even though Callum was now beyond that.

She took a step backwards, eyes never leaving what was left of her friend on the bed, when from the darkness of the bathroom on her left side a figure emerged. It was the man from the mirror. As he appeared, the lights in the hall flickered, as did the lights in the room. He held up his cleaver. It was dripping with blood and viscera.

'Thank you for calling me. I have been asleep for so long. So long. And I am so very, very hungry …'

ABOUT THE AUTHOR

V CASTRO is a two-time Bram Stoker Award nominated author of *Aliens: Vasquez*, *The Haunting of Alejandra*, *The Queen of The Cicadas*, *Goddess of Filth*, *Hairspray and Switchblades*, and *Out of Atzlan*.

She is a Mexican American ex-pat living in the UK for the past 16 years. As a full-time mother, she dedicates her time to her family and writing. She also has a site full of Latinx and merch based on her books - www.lamuertemarket.com

TELL ME I'M SCRUMPTIOUS

OLIVIE BLAKE

It starts when you're functionally a child, unaware of what's happening to your body while you watch his mouth move on screen. You have no prior knowledge of the franchise, which really belongs to the generation preceding yours, before your parents arrived in this country. You sit rapt in the theatre watching his smile, his dimples, the innocence predating the corruption soon to come. For he is a villain, or will be. Not even love can save him; if anything, it dooms him. The scale of the tragedy within the franchise, that pulsating sense of determinism is far more powerful than the writing or really even the acting. It's not a *good* movie, you often say when you're older, once you've aged out of clipping his face from magazines or writing his name in calligraphic script as if it's yours. And true, it's not a good movie. It's almost universally panned, and despite a few other buzzy titles to his name—you watch them all, teenage fantasies playing out in the holo-glow of your lavender-painted bedroom—his career never really takes off. Eventually, you go your separate ways.

By the time you've finished art school and written your first graphic novel to middling success (it's basically fan fiction) and done much better with the second one, such that it gets adapted for the screen, although it's cancelled after one season, you hardly ever think of him. The franchise asks you to be part of a special edition graphic anthology, and of course you joyfully agree. By that time, you've bought your first solo apartment after the divorce and traded your girlhood fantasies for meditation and digestive regularity, which is pretty much the dictionary definition of maturity. It should be the end of your shared story, but it's not.

Because one day you're at a fan convention, at work. They call out his name over the loudspeaker, and something inside you reawakens. You realise with all the nuance of a seizure that you and the object of all your most ardent, innocent fantasies are currently under the same roof.

Which is when it all comes rushing back.

That *guy?* your ex-husband once said with a laugh in his eyes. *Seriously? From the literal worst product of this franchise? Come on, he can barely even act.*

They're not good *movies,* you insisted, stung only a little. *It's just that they're* great *movies.*

Whatever you say, your ex-husband replied. Back when he loved you, or whatever that was.

At the con, you find yourself shocked by what's happening to you bodily just from hearing your teen crush's name. It's been twenty years, probably more, since you last thought of him in a way that felt real, actionable, alive. (Your work is such that you've forgotten these conventions are really a celebration of celebrities, not the little people like you, blithely charting platitudes about the industry for an audience in varying stages of a yawn.)

Your heart does something, it perks up disastrously; you realise you're at work and so is he, and he's in his forties now and you're practically middle-aged and you're stuck at this table with nobody in line to meet you for the next thirty minutes because your publicist told you that's where you're supposed to be. And even if you did decide to get up, gather your things, and sprint across the convention centre to reach him, how exactly would that play out? What could you possibly say? It's not as if they'll let you touch his dimple or lick the side of his face. He's not going to fall in love with you. You're just two adults at work.

So they say last call for the love of your life and you feel that sinking weight, the recurring epiphany of your own irrelevance that you should be well-accustomed to by now. As you always do, you discard it. The fact is, you're extremely competent and talented and, despite everything, you've grown into a person you can be proud of (most days) and anyway, now you're part of the franchise, too. A small piece, a little comic, but the point is you're not the type to go starry-eyed for someone who's just here to collect a per diem and go back home. To wherever he lives. Which is probably Los Angeles, where you also live. To a wife he probably has (a quick Wikipedia search: he's divorced too). You shouldn't meet your heroes anyway. He can't possibly look the same way he did at twenty-one, all bedroom eyes and unrealised evil. You think about the pain in his eyes, the agony that leapt from his (slightly overacted) face to yours through the screen. The perilous, unfaltering depth of his devotion.

You mean nothing to him. How could you ever bear to look him in the eyes and realise in real time just how insignificant you really are? The pain of it collapses your chest, disrupting your remission. No, if the universe had wanted you to meet, you would have known he was going to be here—you would have prepared yourself and planned accordingly, with some semblance of gravitas. But honestly, there's no version of you that handles this with grace. It's the reawakening of your adolescence, all those impulses you learned to repress. Something dormant pokes its head up and you shove it back down, though part of you wants to cry a little. So close, so fucking close you can hardly stand it, so impossibly near it's almost like some tied-up string of fate brought you here—

These are exactly the kinds of thoughts you've grown out of. You shake your head at yourself, text your sister *you'll never believe who's here*. She says *you have to meet him!!!!!!* And you say *come on it's so pathetic it was a million years ago*, but when your signing is over you still wander vaguely in that direction. Just curious, you never know, and anyway, you're just… wandering.

You see the poster with his face, and is it just you or does he kind of look like he's… melting? Bullet dodged, you think. *This way he gets to stay perfect inside my teenage memory* you type out quickly, three words misspelled.

Then you mourn what could have been, and move on.

Until you board your plane and there he is. In first class, of course. You could have sat first class. In fact, you considered it, but the flight is less than two hours and the fact that even you could afford the upgrade made it worthless to you overall. But then there he is, so you lock eyes and look away politely, because he's a human being with a private life and what are you going to do, ask for his autograph? Please. You're both ready to get home.

Still, you can't stop smiling. Looking at him, sneaking glances. Every stage of mania while the person in front of you struggles with the overhead cabin in Comfort Plus. At some point, he catches your smile and smiles back—not really *at* you, you're not egotistical or delusional enough to imagine it could really be that—more so at the fact of you. The knowledge that you're a fan, a person who recognises him. Your existence gives his existence meaning. You think, stupidly: so the universe *did* want us to meet.

The queue progresses, and you consider saying something. Hello, did you enjoy the con? I love you. It's all so ridiculous your smile almost hurts. You soak up one last moment of his proximity and take a step.

A follow-up text to your sister: *nvm he is still hot actually*

You smile some more; a strange, erotic joy.

When it came to your sex life—back when you still had one of those—your husband used to routinely suggest that you were the abnormal one. Never outright, and never in a way you could point to, which served you poorly during counselling, where he grew so adept at highlighting with perfect, irreconcilable clarity his many grievances with the daily burdens of your love. How could you bear it, another thing wrong with you when you were busy trying to fix everything else—your neurotic avoidance of conflict, your bottomless thirst for attention, your unfair demands on his valuable time?

The implication was that your desire was the problem—that you simply had too much *want*, an overactive *need*. You thought his frequency of once a month or so was abnormal, arguably problematic, but the marriage counsellor said to free yourselves from the tyranny of patriarchal constructs, as in what was normal for other couples didn't have to apply to you.

You probably should have known they were sleeping together, but you didn't. You were too busy trying to unscramble the code. To pick the lock and decipher just what it was that was so revolting about you before it was too late, not noticing it was already over until all of a sudden, it was.

By the time you finally deplane, you desperately have to pee. You hold it in favour of getting on the tram to the offsite pick-up zone for rideshares. You're exhausted, you want to get home to your bed. You want to tell someone about your run-in with the galactic emperor, to cultivate the silly little yarn you'll inevitably tell at dinner parties until you die. So you don't initially notice when he falls in step with you, a woman lingering dutifully on his other side.

He's wearing a mask, which is probably how he boarded the plane undetected, but you recognise him by his black baseball cap and the sheer fact of his presence, the way you'd never fail to recognise a man you've wanted to fellate since before you knew what it was to get on your knees. He says: *aren't you that artist who did that comic in that collection?* And yes, it had briefly crossed your mind that he might recognise you if he's ever read any of the graphic versions of his story, but it was so far-fetched an idea that you shook your head and threw it out.

Yes, that was me, you confirm, shocked to be so calm. *And you, of course, are—*

He smiles. *The galaxy's fiercest villain?*

With the galaxy's finest redemption in the end.

Ah, but I never played the redemption role. That was before my time. I was just the corruption part.

His voice is lilting. The woman at his side is sneaking glances at you.

I liked it, you say. *The darkness. You made it complicated. Porous.*

Did I?

The anguish, you incoherently explain. *The rage that came from grief. That it just… that it was all so unselfconscious, the way devotion could be so—*

You stop. This is nonsense.

He smiles.

Jordan, he says to the woman, *is the car here?*

Yes, she says. When you saw her on the plane you thought she was his wife.

Great, he says.

You prepare for a cordial goodbye. You craft something in your head: *obviously you were such a huge part of my life, I'm sure you hear that all the time, but truly you're what brought me to this franchise, I wouldn't be where I am if not for you, I know that's crazy but—*

He looks at you. *Want to get a plate of fries and talk about the cosmos?*

Yes, you say, dazed. You're in a dream. You're a grown woman, so you know this must be something he does all the time, but you can't help it. So what if you're just a notch on the emperor's bedpost? He'll be a notch on yours too. You're not a teenager anymore. There's nothing wrong with this. You know the name of his ex-partner and her entire filmography and he only knows that you like the same movies everyone likes and can draw. But who cares?

So yes, you say. *Definitely.*

Fries go well. So well they lead to drinks. Drinks go very well. Drinks go so well that his assistant goes home in an Uber and he says how about a nightcap and you say yes.

You go to his house, which you're curious about. You're not going to bring up the fact that his IMDB's been vacant since about two years after the franchise ended (you used to rabidly check every chance you could for something new, another opportunity to see him on your screen). He's what the industry calls C-list at this point. So when you pull up to a fancy loft building downtown, you think okay, this is pretty good, it's better than I expected, and then he opens the door to his apartment and you feel surrealism hit you so hard you stop breathing.

Inside is one of those industrial-style interiors. There's no food in the fridge, just three open bottles of wine. He pulls one out and pours. You take it and think: I am alone with you, finally. If past you could only see you now. Who cares that you married the wrong person. It all had to happen to take you to right here, right now.

Come sit, he says. And you do. The couch is nice, it's leather. There's not much personality to anything, except for a few pictures on the TV stand. Which you realise he's not in.

I'm house-sitting for a friend, he says.

Oh, okay.

You both sip your drinks.

I had such a crush on you, you can't help blurting. You can't handle the awkward silence. You want this night to be something—a story, a dream. Anything but nothing, or worse. He smiles and immediately you feel better.

Come here, he says then.

So obviously you do.

Your hands are tied above your head to the pull-up bar in the master bedroom, your heels kicked shoulder-width apart. Your shirt is cropped and he pulls it up with his teeth. He enters you first with his fingers, commandingly. (No need for much foreplay, you've been ready in your imagination for this since you were fifteen.)

It's powerfully erotic, the presence of him, the distinct aura of masculinity and convention hotel soap. He fills you and you cry out for more, please, more.

Call me the emperor, a hot grunt in your ear. Fuck yes. The fantasy completed, like a prophecy fulfilled, brings you soaring over the edge of your climax.

My lord, you whisper to the span of his shoulder, once he's loosed your wrists and caught you boneless in his arms. *You make galaxies crumble.*

Before you know it, he's ready to go again.

You keep seeing each other. More often than you responsibly should, because you have a deadline and you can already feel the carpal tunnel coming on. But how can you resist this? You call him His Lordship from a place of carnality and immediately, it sticks. He's in your phone as the emperor. You text him: *Your Lordship, I'll be on my knees for you in five.* He hearts the message.

You show up and he's wearing the outfit. The one from the scene in the second film where he breaks down confessing his crimes to his lover, the galactic fucking do-gooder who marries him in secret and then dies of a broken heart. Dumb bitch. You would never. The cosplay is so real, fake blood smeared across his cheek, his hair—thinner now than it was—tumbling into the sweat on his forehead. He breaks down in your arms. *I killed them all. I killed them.*

Shhhh, you say, holding him. *Shhhhh. I've got you. I see your darkness. I do not fear it.*

(The film dialogue: *Oh ______, what have you done?)*

He looks you in the eyes with something deeper than adoration. Awe?

Then you fuck for so long you almost lose your voice to screams.

Your husband never liked your penchant for fantasy. He made you feel like you were weird. But now, finally, you can guiltlessly ask yourself: why was it weird to want to suck off the giant cock of the galaxy's hottest emperor? Of course it tasted better to pretend, to grip a vessel of true power. Nobody wants to fuck the webmaster of some fucking website. That's nobody's fantasy. We all want to get railed by a dick of significance. Absolute power corrupts absolutely. It also gives head like a motherfucking dream.

In the comic you wrote for the franchise, the emperor relives his moments of regret and concludes he regrets nothing. He had a darkness no woman could love but that every creature in the universe respected. What would goodness have offered him that could ever compare except for the mundanity of taxes, marriages ending and futures collapsing, doing your little diets and drawing your little pictures like an accolade might finally make you sexy enough—a life wishing endlessly and pointlessly on stars? So what if they called you evil. At least they called you something. At least they looked at you at all.

After about a month, you show up at his place and buzz to be let in as you've done every night for the last several weeks. This time, though, he doesn't answer. You type *??* into your phone and he texts you *sorry, forgot to say I'm back home now.* Okay, where's home? He gives you the address in Silverlake, whatever, back in the car. You show up and it's an apartment on the bottom floor of a small-ish building, about six units. You knock. He answers.

Your Lordship, you say. He gives you the kind of kiss that transmits hot ore down the sexy flimsy of your panties. By necessity, this is the only reality you can cling to. If you look too closely at the details you might see something you don't like.

It's a one-bedroom apartment with clothes everywhere. It smells a little bit like varnish, a sour waft of disrepair. He puts your face to the headboard while he fucks you, so temporarily you lose interest in matters of interior design. But then you go to the bathroom afterward and register in a way you can't quite come back from that this apartment belongs to a man.

You go back out to the emperor of emperors, king of kings,

and settle yourself on your knees while he opens a beer you haven't touched since college. He spreads his legs and you fit yourself between them. He caresses your hair. You close your eyes.

He kisses you hard. *Do you know how special you are to me?*

You shiver at the prospect of it. Your specialness. You allow it to reconfigure your sanity, to shape the constraints of calculations you've been making in your mind.

Am I, my lord?

Don't tease me.

I'm not. I wouldn't.

Everyone in my life is so fucking shitty. He looks away, restless.

You place a kiss in the middle of his palm. *They just don't see how powerful you are.*

He looks back at you then.

Don't fuck with me.

I'm not.

You're serious?

You don't like how much reassurance he expects you to give him. The emperor of the galaxy shouldn't need this much emotional labour, but fine.

Yes my lord, of course. You're my king of kings. You stand up and wiggle out of your underwear again. *Make me beg for you.*

When you lower yourself onto him he groans raggedly, his head cresting the edge of the couch. There's a stain on the cushion and you almost remember that he has earned nothing in recent years aside from merchandise royalties and paid appearances at low-level cons. But thankfully your mind recalls the fanatics, the lines of people desperate for a chance to breathe his air. Yes. There. Better.

You ride the emperor of the galaxy until he turns to jelly between your thighs. You did that. It's real. You have power over him and he, in turn, is power absolute. That is yours, which no one can take from you.

You can shape it, reality, if you really try. What's real is simply what you accept. The couples counsellor who fucked your husband was right about one thing: normal isn't a scale worth determining. Any person is always just a person. You can rewrite yourself for a man, but he'll still betray you, so in a way, deviating from the fantasy is a betrayal in itself. Eventually you just have to be done apologising for who you used to be. Who you are.

It's my agent, the emperor murmurs to you with a long-suffering sigh, his fingers tracing patterns on your spine. *He's up my ass about reading some fucking Z-lister's script.*

You could tell him money is money. That he's not exactly in a position to choose. But for him to accept this, you must accept it first, and none of this makes sense if you change the story even a little bit.

You should punish him.

What?

You're the emperor. Not him. He answers to you. You shrug as if to say, isn't it obvious?

He searches your face with curiosity. His eyes are deep with it, the desperation to know with soulful certainty that he's not alone. You gaze at each other with perfect understanding then. Together you cross over into the fantasy, or so it feels to you at the time.

He flips you onto your back and you feel a sock underneath you. Unimportant. You taste the beer on his breath. He is so tormented, your lord. It's so hard to rule the galaxy. So stressful to be torn in two by the agony of trauma and ambition. All that rage and longing and sex.

Come with me, he whispers. His tongue threads the lips of your precious chosen cunt. All the cunts in all the galaxy. The king of kings has chosen yours.

Yes, you say, *my lord, of course.*

The house in Beverly Hills is comically large, truly laughable. Of course a usurper lives in a castle while the true heir sits in Silverlake and starves. Of course a man who pretends at the throne must live as if his life is perpetually at risk. He may have his loyal guards, his threats of ADT protection and neighbourhood watch, but why should any of that scare you? The galaxy hangs in the balance. You must restore the natural order. Your oppression under the regime of the pretender is the crime that really counts.

You finger the curve of your blaster, dauntlessly pushing your way inside. The enemy wants you subjugated, but this is what revolution is, the necessity of righteousness. Power is a matter of destiny, of bending the outcome to your will. You feel your lordship's power radiating from him, the heat of your lover's fierceness, as you take the battlefield at last.

You enter the arena together, your fate hand in hand with your doom. (Not really, of course. In the films the emperor dies, but not this way.) By now, reality is this: you will die at his side rather than surrender. Even when he smells like B.O. and unwashed feet, you still choose the love story. And in the story you have chosen, this is fucking sex itself.

In the news, they will say things like ONE-HIT WONDER AND DERANGED FAN COMMIT MURDER SPREE WITH ILLUSTRATED MANIFESTO, with sensational half-truths like FORMER FACE OF FRANCHISE KNOWN TO HAVE BATTLED ADDICTION ISSUES FOR YEARS. There will be suggestions of bath salts and fentanyl, any meaningless cornucopia of drugs. FRIENDS OF THE ARTIST SAY SIGNS OF INSTABILITY WERE ALWAYS THERE, that's an easy one.

FORMER HUSBAND SAYS 'SHE ALWAYS WANTED ME TO DRESS UP LIKE A F***ING SERIAL KILLER,' and, 'THE INTERNET ROTTED HER BRAIN.'

They won't publish the manifesto you wrote and illustrated, which is a shame because it's beautiful. In it you look fifteen and full of moxie. Your tits are perfect and you don't have hips and the light hasn't yet left your eyes. Likewise, your lordship has that undeniable smile, that playful recklessness that gives way to wretchedness in his terrible, Shakespearean turn of despair.

The tragedy of the franchise is written so deep in the bone—the tragedy being that from inside the story, nobody could change it. The ending was already predetermined. The marriage was doomed, but you didn't know it. It didn't have to happen this way, but you couldn't have done anything differently, so it did.

When the bodies lie still and cold on the floor and you breathlessly look your emperor in the eye, you tell yourself you will not see doubt this time, nor any trace of accusation. You will see only togetherness, completion. This, the act of communion! You expect him to press you backward into the mattress, to wipe away the smear of blood on your mouth with his thumb. The spoils of loyal service should be this: eternal tenderness and devotion.

My lord, you will say, as the first of the police sirens wail.

But instead he says your name, which isn't the right dialogue. Meanwhile, he's panting like a fucking dog. He's saying *fuck fuck fuck what have you done what have you done oh my god*. He smells like rancid sweat and piss and it's embarrassing, the way he tries to break free of the fantasy now, when it's too late. The manifesto's already been written.

My lord, you say, more sternly, as if to wake him from a dream, but he's not listening.

FUCK, he says. He's panicking as if he's never massacred an entire planetary system before. *Ohhhhhh my fucking god. What did you do? I thought we were just—I thought we were only going to* scare *him a little—*

My lord, please. The galaxy—

Would you fucking stop that for a second I know it's hot but this is real life okay. This is not some fucking movie I was in a hundred years ago. Are you insane?

He looks at you. You let your disapproval show.

Wait, he says. *Wait. Oh my god. Oh god. You actually* are *insane, aren't you?*

Get it together, you snap. *You're the emperor. You should be thanking me right now. You should be bathing in the blood of your enemies, okay? Jesus. Grow the fuck up.*

You're telling me *to grow up?*

(Your ex said this to you before he left. That you live in a constant fantasy. That you want him to be something he isn't. That you want your marriage to be something it's not. He says this to you and then he leaves with that bitch he's been fucking, the one you knew he was fucking but you told yourself adults didn't search each other's emails or text messages and so you didn't even try to look for proof. And then *he* said grow up, you only write comics because you've been frozen at fifteen for halfway to forever. Because he thinks you're the one who's broken. Not him, who apparently can't be faulted for not sticking to a vow.)

Look okay I'll make some calls. Okay? I'll get you a good lawyer I swear. I just never thought… I just really didn't think this would get so out of hand okay well never mind we have to get out of here we have to burn these clothes we have to—oh my god what am I going to say to his kids my career is fucking finished I was supposed to do an audition next week for M. Night Shyamalan's new thing—

My lord, you say calmly. But he doesn't look at you, not right away.

I'm supposed to be having a fucking renaissance right now! Nostalgia's back, I mean—I'm supposed to be out here, fucking... I don'tknow,shootingflashbacksforDisneyorsomeshit—FUCK,Ijustcan't—

You take a step then, and now he sees you.

Finally.

What are you doing? Why are you looking at me like that?

He blinks. *Stop, stop looking at me like that—Babe—*

My love, you correct him. *You say 'my love', and you beg for my forgiveness. You get on your knees before me and you pray for absolution.*

Okay, okay—

Stop crying.

I'm not, I'm sorry—

You're the fucking emperor. Don't fucking cry.

I'm not, I'm just... I just—please, please don't—

Just then it dawns on you. Of course! You're in *the usurper's house*. Of course he has some kind of protective ward that means everyone who enters is transformed. This is not your emperor. This is not the man who laid waste to cities for you, for the honour of your love. Clever usurper.

Now you smile.

Goodbye, you say to the man who is not the emperor, just a guy in his forties who is not even a very good actor and who definitely has veneers. Thank God you can see things plainly now. Because when the smoke clears, you will know only this: that your true emperor will find you. After all, the universe willed it once. Even the galaxy isn't boundless. He is searching for you, and you for him, and however long it takes, you will find each other.

The story you accept is this: Your love will be regarded with honour again, someday.

Then you pull the trigger on your blaster, and you mourn what could have been.

ABOUT THE AUTHOR

OLIVIE BLAKE, the pen name of Alexene Farol Follmuth, is the author of bestselling fantasy and sci-fi crossover titles for adults. She is a lover and writer of stories, many of which involve the fantastic, the paranormal, or the supernatural, but not always. More often, her works revolve around the collective experience, what it means to be human (or not), and the endlessly interesting complexities of life and love.

Olivie tripped and fell into writing after abandoning her long-premeditated track for Optimum Life Achievement while attending law school, and now focuses primarily on the craft and occasional headache of creating fiction. Her *New York Times* and *Sunday Times* bestselling *The Atlas Six* released 2022 from Tor Books, rounding out the bestselling trilogy with *The Atlas Paradox* and *The Atlas Complex* in 2024. The re-release of her viral literary romance *Alone With You in the Ether* was followed by backlist titles *One for My Enemy* and *New York Times* bestselling *Masters of Death*, with brand new titles *Gifted & Talented* and *Girl Dinner* to release in 2025. She has also been published as the writer for the graphic series *Clara and the Devil* and a variety of other adult SFF books. As Alexene, she is the author of young adult fiction (alexenefarolfollmuth.com).

Olivie lives and works in Los Angeles with her husband and goblin prince/toddler.

ABOUT THE AUTHOR

THE COMPENSATION

RAMSEY CAMPBELL

When the airline representative read out Vi's name, Desmond stood up as well. 'I'm afraid that's the last seat today, Mrs Princely,' the rep, Jeanette, said.

'In that case we'll both wait.'

As the woman seated opposite the Princelys in the airport concourse slapped her knees in preparation for taking Vi's place, Desmond said, 'You go home to the little ones while you've got the chance, Vi. They'll be missing us.'

'How soon would he be able to come home, Jeanette?'

'Our next flight out will be tomorrow.' Over a widespread murmur of dissatisfaction, the rep said, 'We can guarantee seats for everybody here who unfortunately can't fly today. We've booked you all into a hotel, and we've arranged an activity for anyone who'd like one.'

'See, Vi? I'll be taken care of. You needn't worry about me.'

'I'll do my best.' She left him with a fierce hug and swift kiss. 'I'll let you know how we get on,' she said.

'Maybe keep it short, though. We don't know how much calls may cost round here.'

As Vi trundled her suitcase to the security gates, the woman she'd denied a seat said, 'How old are your children?'

'We've none of those. I didn't have it in me,' Desmond added in the hope that sympathy might outweigh any resentment at the misunderstanding. 'My wife's going home to our three terriers.'

'We all have our priorities,' the woman said, twisting the ends of the souvenir scarf she wore. 'Mine's my aging mother.'

Guilt might have prompted him to call Vi back if she hadn't passed through security. 'If you'd all like to follow me,' Jeanette said, 'I'll take you to your hotel.'

A coach piebald with mud was parked outside the cramped airport. Above a relatively clear arc of the windscreen a matrix sign displayed a word in characters Desmond had no time to decipher. Before he could intervene, the driver of the coach used the telescopic handle to swing his case into the luggage compartment, and Desmond could only clamber aboard the coach. A highway apparently untrammelled by a speed limit brought the coachload to a city crammed with flat grey elongated blocks that poked out apartment balconies above single-windowed shops and restaurants. The narrow streets did little to restrain the mass of dented traffic braying like the stampede it aspired to achieve. The coach set half its wheels on several pavements on its way to the hotel, a grey hulk distinguished only by a cast-iron awning that had splashed rusty stains across the pavement underneath. If Desmond read the insecure tipsy letters on the awning right, the hotel went by the name of Golob. At least the square in front of it excluded traffic apart from the coach. He was in time to grab his case by the proper handle before following Jeanette into the hotel.

The concrete lobby was just large enough to accommodate the newcomers. Legless benches stuck out from three of the unadorned walls. A flag bearing the motif Desmond had seen on the woman's scarf—a fist clasping a bolt of lightning separated from a helmet that might house a head—occupied the wall above a mass of keys on hooks behind a rudimentary counter. The receptionist, a woman with a high forehead comically emulated by her chin, sent the new arrivals a look that stopped well short of welcoming. 'Who'd like a tour of the town?' Jeanette said.

'We haven't even got our rooms yet,' the woman with the scarf complained.

'All taken care of for you, and anyone who wants the walking tour can join it in an hour. Just make sure it's the English-language tour. Show the guide your boarding card and there won't be any charge. All the tours meet in the square outside, by the statue of the Supreme.'

Desmond couldn't contain his snort at this. The receptionist seized both her ears and raised her head, apparently to establish what she'd heard, while Jeanette looked away from the gesture and frowned at him. 'Were you wanting to say something, Mr Princely?'

'It sounds as if they've put up a statue of someone out of an old rock band.'

'I wouldn't joke about the ruler while you're a guest in his country. Some people mightn't be too happy.' She sent the receptionist an apologetic grimace. 'Now let's see what accommodation we have for you,' she said.

She didn't mean Desmond by any means immediately. When at last he heard his name the receptionist threw a key on the counter with a thud like the slamming of a lid. The key was shackled to a tarnished metal club several times its size. The three digits on the club led him up several flights of chipped concrete stairs and down a dim, unembellished corridor to a room that shared with its neighbour whatever there was in the way of a bathroom. The narrow single bed severely packaged in a frayed white sheet left barely enough space for him to struggle past the shallow wardrobe and token chest of drawers to the window. The cracked pane showed him dozens of similar windows embedded in concrete, while the apartment opposite could have been reflecting an empty version of his room. He dumped his case on top of the chest and took photographs of the room to show Vi once he was home.

He was crossing the lobby when the receptionist knocked on the counter and twisted her other hand in the air, apparently demanding the key Desmond was glad to relinquish. In the square Desmond examined the statue while he waited for the tour. The faceless stone figure that stood on the plinth was practically abstract apart from the lightning bolt in its fingerless fist. Cannonballs surrounded its heavy boots, and Desmond read the plaque on the plinth as saying SUPROMOCH. He guessed the facelessness conveyed that the status was more important than the person, no doubt a tenet of the national politics. He hoisted himself to sit on the edge of the plinth while his fellow tourists began wandering out of the hotel.

They looked determined to make the best of the situation, which had nearly gone so well. The travel firm hadn't collapsed during his and Vi's fortnight away, and no passengers had caused the flights to be aborted. No airport staff had gone on strike, and no protesters had hindered the holiday. Just a glitch in a computer system had caused widespread diversions, stranding Vi and Desmond's flight in a country they had never heard of.

The tour guide was plainly local: peaked forehead dividing a fall of straight grey hair, small face cramped by brows and long chin. 'You will see our city,' she announced, less in the manner of promising a treat than Desmond thought appropriate. Once she'd stared at the boarding cards from the diverted flight, she turned towards the side of the square opposite the route the coach had taken. 'You will follow me,' she said.

Vi would have shared a grin at the guide's style with Desmond, if not surreptitious mirth. Perhaps some of the party straggling across the square did so, but they weren't including him. He stayed beside the woman with the scarf until her hostile glances made him fall behind as they reached an undistinguished street that sloped towards a distant river. The guide hurried down it to a corner where a man was squatting in a ragged sack. Desmond was the last to pass him, and the man stretched out a trembling hand to him.

The hand and the elongated face poking out of the sack that must do duty as a bed were starved virtually to the bone. Whatever words the man was wailing, there was no mistaking the appeal. As Desmond dug in his pocket, he felt delegated to make up for everybody who had hastened past without donating. He planted several euros and smaller coins in the outstretched hand. They jittered and jangled until the man finished peering at them, and then he flung them across the street and spat after them. 'Can't you spend those here?' Desmond protested. 'They're all I can offer.'

Even if he'd succeeded in communicating regret, he couldn't miss the tone of the response. He backed away from the man, whose bagged body had begun to jerk like a contestant in a sack race. Most of the coins had escaped the onslaught of sputum. As Desmond finished retrieving those he saw a woman glaring disapproval at him from an upper window. He threw his arms wide to mime helplessness, which seemed doubly appropriate when he realised the tour he'd been following was nowhere to be seen or heard. 'Where have they gone?' he blurted.

He was hoping that the watcher up above might point the way, but she turned her back. He sprinted to a crossroads boxed in by apartment blocks and saw the scarved woman several hundred yards away, vanishing past a bend. He was in time to catch up with her at yet another corner, from which he saw the guided tour ahead. All the women were wearing the identical scarf, some of them around their heads, and the pole the male guide was brandishing bore the national emblem as well. The woman Desmond had pursued was someone he'd never seen before, and the guide was addressing the small procession in the local language. 'Excuse me,' Desmond called, 'where's the English tour?'

The parade and its leader swung around to gaze at him. Every head sported the style of face and chin he'd come to recognise, and just the features varied, if not too much. The guide had fallen silent, and nobody else spoke. 'English?' Desmond pleaded.

They greeted this with smiles and a burst of applause, followed by a concerted gesture urging him to join the tour. It felt more welcoming than the one he'd lost, and he assumed it would return to the square outside the hotel. The guide wasn't simply beckoning to him but indicating a doorway surmounted by an outthrust representation of a tankard. Perhaps the bar was the first attraction offered by the tour.

The long dim narrow room led beneath low rough beams to a counter. Members of the tour stood around circular tables, and Desmond might have thought more of the party were crouching behind the bar. The faces grinning at him over it belonged to a line of tall capacious tankards that displayed the national characteristics, as everybody in the room did expect for Desmond. The tour guide brought him a tankard that could have won a contest for mirth, and the barman filled the popeyed china mug to the brim from the last of the sizeable barrels he bore with no visible effort around the room. Desmond might have felt isolated, having had to find space at a table by himself, if all the diners hadn't raised their gleeful tankards to him. 'Cheers,' he said, elevating his own.

The word everybody chorused in response sounded close to the name of his hotel. The golden ale tasted sweeter than he was used to, but a couple of mouthfuls increased its appeal. Draining the tankard earned him a round of applause, and the barman refilled the mug at once, though from a different barrel. The contents were more honeyed still, which took little time to appeal to him. Presumably his fellow topers found the style less attractive, since they declined the offer of the barrel. As Desmond emptied the tankard again the guide said, 'Supromoch.'

The drinkers set their tankards down with a concerted thump that resounded through the room. Desmond's belated bid to join in earned him a unanimous stare that left him wondering if he'd presumed too much. When the party trooped out he hurried in their wake, down to a square hemmed in by identical apartments. Except for the absence of a hotel, he could have mistaken it for its predecessor.

No, the statue wasn't quite the same. While the figure had yet to admit to a face, the objects clustering around its feet no longer looked entirely like cannonballs. While the vague depressions they exhibited put Desmond in mind of finger holes, could that really be a ring of bowling balls? As he squinted at them in a bid to dismiss the dullness that the ale had settled on his brain, he realised everybody else was circling the monument. The leisurely parade resembled a slowed-down dance, if not a ritual, not least since every head was lowered—every eye as well. He thought it best to duck his head, not too tardily, he hoped. No sooner had he done so than the guide uttered a collection of untranslated syllables, and everyone stepped back from the plinth.

The tour had reached the older section of the town. While the blocks that flanked the downhill slope stayed grey and continued to hulk, they were carved with images above a multitude of doors:

swords, axes, protruding heads reminiscent of gargoyles but presumably denoting some historic ownership. An occasional living counterpart craned over one of the balconies that sprouted from apartments, but it must be the ale that made Desmond wonder if the applause that rained down was meant for him. The guide had reached another corner. 'Supromoch,' he said.

From the corner Desmond saw a square at the foot of a street, halfway down which a man was standing in a doorway in the middle of a block. Although the guide strode past with the barest glance, Desmond could have taken the room beyond the doorway for a folk museum representing some local way of life. The entire far wall of the large gloomy room was covered by the national flag, in front of which three heads poked over the edge of a table set with china bearing the same emblem. He had to squint to establish that the heads weren't tankards but belonged to children lined up on a bench like a display set up for anybody passing to appreciate. Beside the table an old woman was sitting just as still in a paralysed rocking chair. Her head was bent as if the burden of her chin had weighed it down, but she lifted it to greet Desmond, though the gesture needed both hands to aid it. If her toothless cackle contained a pair of syllables, he couldn't be certain he recognised them. Was the man in the doorway nodding at him or her or both? Desmond was too busy following the guide to judge, especially once he saw the next monument ahead.

This one was making itself clearer. While the figure with a handful of a storm persisted in keeping its face to itself, its feet were surrounded by stylised heads, as jocund as any of the tankards in the bar. The guide and his bowed imitators were plodding around the plinth, and Desmond sensed their eyes on him despite their stance. He felt urged, if not compelled, to join them, and two women made space for him. Perhaps the ale was catching up with him, since he'd begun to grow dizzy by the time he felt allowed to lift his head.

The next street continued downhill. They must surely be close to the river, even if he couldn't see it for the maze the old town was. By no means all the heads the buildings thrust out above the street were carved. Many of the balconies were occupied, and more watchers were emerging further down the slope. Was the tour such an uncommon sight, or were they meant to add to the experience somehow? Their silence seemed to gather on him, so that he couldn't help feeling watched. On the whole he was glad when the guide broke the silence at the far end of the street with the apparently inevitable word.

Signs made it plain that all four sides of the square consisted of office blocks. All the workers seemed to be taking a break, unless they'd been sent out by some kind of alarm, since the edges of the square were a mass of men and women dressed in suits too drab for anything but work. They watched the tour converge on the central monument, where Desmond kept his head as low as anyone's, having seen that the objects clustered on the plinth looked not just grotesquely cheerful but proud of their state. The victim indicated by the lightning bolt appeared to feel especially honoured. As Desmond fell to pacing around the plinth it occurred to him that the guide had hardly spoken apart from the announcement he kept making. How much of a tour was this supposed to be? It had begun to feel more like a ceremonial procession. Perhaps he hadn't joined a tour at all.

He stumbled out of the downcast parade and tried to steady his stagger across the square towards the street he'd most recently descended, only to realise he couldn't remember the rest of the route. The ale had doused his memory, and he appealed to the nearest group of office workers as best he could. 'Golob?'

'Golob.'

The man Desmond had nearly floundered against repeated the word, and then his colleagues did. They must work in a large office, given their number. Perhaps their grins were meant to put Desmond at his ease rather than comment on his perfunctory usage, and their laughter too. He didn't really need their neighbours on both sides to take up the chant and the other reactions as well. Indeed, it sounded as if all these were making their way around the square, and he could only hope somebody would be able to point out his route. When the people he was facing gazed beyond him as if the answer had arrived, he turned to find the guide at his back. 'Golob,' the guide declared.

Perhaps tours were conducted differently here. Its failure to conform to Desmond's expectations needn't mean it wasn't one, and besides, he assumed the guide was undertaking to deliver him back to the hotel in due course. The crowd moved apart to clear the exit the man was heading for, and Desmond saw onlookers blocking the entrance the party had used. Surely this oughtn't to bother him, and he was first to follow the guide.

Every balcony on both sides of the downhill slope was occupied, by silence too. The only noises were Desmond's footsteps and the guide's and those behind them, which the narrow street seemed to multiply. On the right-hand side the balconies gave out ahead of the next corner, and the separated block that led there appeared to lack windows as well. The guide halted as he reached it. 'Supromoch,' he declared and took hold of a heavy brass handle to ease the door open beneath a high, rounded arch.

The building was a church, or had been, but every window was painted as black as the bricks. The interior wasn't much less bare than any of the squares: not a pew or an altar to be seen, and not much light either. A version of the omnipresent monument stood in the middle of the stone floor. 'Supromoch,' the guide repeated in little more than a whisper, indicating the plinth with a nod that resembled the start of an obeisance.

As his followers crowded into the dimness they made a gesture Desmond couldn't fathom. While it reminded him of the woman in the rocking chair, their exaggerated version could hardly be doing their necks much good. What was different about the figure on the plinth? The jagged knife-edged bolt it held sent the visitors a metallic glint, but what was the figure composed of? The meagre glow the windows and doorway admitted let him discern the man had some kind of face—certainly teeth bared in a smile related to a snarl. There were faces at his feet as well, but if they had ever displayed satisfaction at their state, some process had subsequently warped their looks. Desmond was about to venture closer, beckoned with increasing vigour by the guide, when the last of the newcomers closed the door.

It shut out too much of the grudging light, along with the voiceless sounds of a crowd that must have followed the party out of the square. Desmond was still able to distinguish the devotees making for the plinth as if they were drawn to it by their lowered outthrust heads. The murk that smelled musty if not worse left him reluctant to imitate them, and so did their dogged ritualistic behaviour. He was preparing to force himself to join in, if only so as not to attract attention he feared he wouldn't welcome, when he heard a whisper. 'Doesn't hurt.'

If this might have been addressed to him, the response seemed not to be. 'Doesn't hurt us.'

So they'd understood him more than they pretended, and what else might they have feigned? As he made to speak, his phone rang. 'Vi,' it said in the midst of shrilling.

Every head jerked up except for the ones on the plinth, a

reaction so violent that Desmond retreated to the wall furthest from the door. The instant he cut off the ringtone Vi said, 'I looked it up and this isn't costing us too much. I just wanted to hear your voice.'

Desmond kept it down as he turned to the wall. 'Where are you?'

'We've just touched down at home. How about you? I hope you're out and about.'

'I've been on a tour of the town. I'm in some kind of church.'

'Don't let me disturb anybody, then. Have the best time you can and send me a message when you know when you'll be flying.'

'I'll do all that. I—' Before he could say goodbye or more than that, the call was dead. As he pocketed the phone a voice said, 'Better than a church.'

Was that the guide? Had he pretended not to understand English too? Desmond was turning to confront him when he realised the voice had come from somewhere above the visitors, and then another observation caught up with him: theirs hadn't been the only reactions he'd glimpsed to the phone call. As if the recognition had lent it more life, the figure they surrounded moved again. It kicked away one of the tributes, which flew off the bench.

The object struck the floor with a hollow bony thud and rolled within inches of Desmond. Even in the dimness he couldn't have taken it for a sculpture, especially given the grimace the jaw dislocated by the impact was sending him. Gloom had replaced its eyes, and he was more than glad not to see the face in greater detail. Now it was his turn to pretend—to behave as if everything, or at any rate enough, were normal, or that he hadn't noticed the reverse. 'I'll wait outside till you've finished,' he said as steadily as his unstable mouth could manage, and set about sidling along the wall. When all the votaries pacing around the plinth raised their heads he could only desperately hope it was part of the rite, particularly since they were lifting them so high—too high, he could have thought, for their bodies to accommodate. He didn't want to think the action was a way of searching for him in the dimness, but still less did he care to fancy they were miming how he might be added to the plinth. 'I'm not from here,' he pleaded in a voice that barely struggled between his unwieldy lips, and wondered too late if he was condemning himself.

ABOUT THE AUTHOR

RAMSEY CAMPBELL celebrated his 60th anniversary of his debut publishing in 2024. The Oxford Companion to English Literature describes him as 'Britain's most respected living horror writer'. He has been given more awards than any other writer in the field, including the Grand Master Award of the World Horror Convention, the Lifetime Achievement Award of the Horror Writers Association, the Living Legend Award of the International Horror Guild and the World Fantasy Lifetime Achievement Award. In 2015 he was made an Honorary Fellow of Liverpool John Moores University for outstanding services to literature. PS Publishing have brought out Phantasmagorical Stories in two volumes, a sixty-year retrospective of his short stories, as well as *Six Stooges and Counting*, a personal appreciation of the comedy team. *The Incubations* and his Brichester Mythos trilogy are his latest from Flame Tree Press. As part of the 2025 World Fantasy Convention programme, Ramsey will be celebrated as their Horror Laureate, tying in with their '50 Years of British Fantasy and Horror' theme. Born in Liverpool in 1946, he now lives in Wallasey, and continues to write horror.

ABOUT THE AUTHOR

THE OTHER BROTHER

RIAN HUGHES

PROLOGUE

'*This is the book!* The one I was telling you about, remember? The one that disturbed me so much I had to bury it!'

Mia was pointing up at the 'Old and Interesting' shelf behind the till. Isaac hoped the label was a guide to the books filed there rather than the audience to which they might appeal. 'There. Far left.'

It certainly didn't look like anything special. The spine had come away at the top, the remaining piece holding on by a loose web of stringy buckram and providence. He sympathised.

'How did you spot that? I can't read the title—'

'*Isaac.*' Her schoolteacherly reprimand suggested the answer should be obvious. 'I recognise the colour, the size. That's how these things work. It's not just the *story* you recall, it's the way it's *presented*. The whole package. The texture of the paper, the binding, the *smell*—'

Her finger hovered over the top for a hesitant second, then pulled the slim volume towards her.

Looking at Isaac rather than her discovery, she held it between her palms so the cover was obscured; a pause before the anticipated reveal. An apologetic smile pulled at her cheek. 'Look, it probably wasn't that well written. I'm not claiming this is great literature or anything, some lost classic. But I didn't know that. It was all new to me – even derivative third-rate stories can be box-fresh originals for someone, somewhere.'

'Everyone has to have a first time sometime.' Isaac put the copy of *The Story of O* he'd been contemplating buying back on the shelf.

'*Right.*'

'And even if it was dreadful, we still remember it years later. That's how nostalgia works. So what's it about? Show me!'

Mia raised her hand like a waiter lifting a silver cloche. First impressions weren't that scintillating, Isaac had to admit. The cover was printed duotone, a sage green and Prussian blue on what would have been cream linen before age and sun toasted it to a warm umber round the edges. Across the top in ornate art nouveau lettering was written the title: *The Other Brother*, by P. K. Meek, and below that was a scratchy line drawing of a small child whose shorts were supported by braces fitted with comically large buttons. 'P. K. Meek? Should I have heard of him? Her?'

Isaac narrowed his eyes to bring them into focus. Behind the diminutive figure, an ill-defined dark shape loomed up like an amorphous cloud. It might have been his shadow, cast up the wall and onto the ceiling by the candle he was holding, save for the fact it had two thin eyes and a long curling mouth shaped not unlike the curling piece of spine. It hunched over the child, a suggestion of thin talons forming a nested parenthesis around his head.

The boy – the brother of the title? – appeared to be unconcerned by this shadow presence behind him. Perhaps it was his pet, or a figment of his imagination.

'How old did you say you were when you read this?'

'Nine. Ten, maybe.' Mia tilted her head. 'I clearly remember when and where I found it. Friends of the family had a summer cottage in Rye, near Dungeness. It was in a small alcove, under a stack of Ordnance Survey maps and theatre programmes. I took it without asking. I didn't think anyone would miss it.'

'But you buried it, you said?'

Mia hesitated. 'Yes.' She'd dropped her voice to a whisper. 'In the field adjoining my Aunt Felicity's back garden. I put it in an old box file, then dug a small trench with a spoon, as Dad had done when he buried our cat. Then I trod it down and sprinkled willow leaves and moss over to hide the spot. I washed the spoon clean under the tap in the sideway, dried it on the corner of my dress and put it back in the cutlery drawer. I didn't want anyone to know what I'd done. Why did I—' She ducked her head and looked embarrassed. 'An exorcism, I guess. I just didn't want it in the house. Like I said. It— it disturbed me.'

'You *have* to get it! I'll buy it for you.'

'Really?'

'Unless you're still frightened of an old children's story, of course—'

'No, no. Ha. Of course I'm not.'

'Then pass it over.' Isaac thumbed open the cover. A price was pencilled on the half title. '*Ah*. Ok, I guess this is an early birthday present.'

Mia watched him negotiate the ill-packed shelves and stacks and boxes back to the desk at the front of the shop. Particles of airborne woodpulp pirouetted in the sunlight shafting through the front windows as Isaac said something inaudible to the cashier, who nodded, put the book in a paper bag with 'Otter Books' stamped on the front, then held out a card reader. Isaac tapped it with his phone and it emitted an incongruous beep. Surely she could program that thing to imitate the analogue ring of a vintage till, Mia thought. Atmosphere. It's all in the details.

I

THE PAPER bag was now on the bedside table, under the repro Tiffany lamp with the broken pane. Mia saw it and stopped, one leg in her pyjama trousers, the other hovering midair. Isaac looked at her, at the table, laughed, then rolled over and picked it up. 'I'm going to read it to you. A chapter every night.'

'Really?'

'Why not? It'll be fun.' He tipped up the bag and slid the book out, then held it under his nose. '*Mmm.* See how much of it you remember. No peeking.'

'Book sniffer.'

'Ha.'

'Old and stinky. Just like you.' Mia pulled her pyjamas up, tied the cord, then pulled the top tight across her chest. There was a short pause. 'What if it gives me nightmares?'

Isaac snorted. 'Mia, *I'm* here. I'm your hero, ta da.' He flexed an entirely imaginary bicep. 'I'll protect you.'

'From what? The Other Brother?'

Isaac looked at the cover. 'Is that him? I have no idea who the bad guy is here.' Mia was still standing by the bed, arms folded. Isaac patted the blankets beside him. 'So what was it, exactly, about this story that disturbed you?'

'*Pffft.* You'll think I'm silly. It's not a particularly gory story, if I recall. But … Tomas, that's the boy on the cover – well, somehow this Other Brother takes the place of his real brother, Elias. But no one else seems to notice. Tomas is the only one that knows. He can't persuade anyone that anything is amiss. So he sets out to trick this Other Brother into revealing himself, but he knows everything his real brother would have known – birthdays, the names of their friends, where the plasticine is kept in the church hall, memories of obscure events no one else could know about. And after a while he begins to wonder whether he is the one who is mistaken.

'And that's what I found so disturbing – the idea that someone close to you, your brother or mother or father or sister might be … something else. *Someone* else. Something *pretending* to be someone you know. Something which has snuck into your most private spaces and taken up residence – and however much you protest, no one will believe you.'

'What you're describing – that sounds a bit like a real medical condition, Mia. I can't remember the name, but – *bash*. A knock to the head, and you think everyone close to you is now a lifelike robot duplicate, or an actor on the payroll of the CIA or the Secret Service.'

Mia rolled into bed and kicked the blanket up so it resettled across the two of them. 'Whatever. I was *nine* remember? Giving it some official medical term wouldn't have made me feel any better.'

Isaac ran the flat of his thumbnail along the spine to see if he could even it out, but only succeeded in breaking a centimetre off the end. He surreptitiously dropped it in the cold cup of tea on the bedside table, then looked across at Mia without moving his head. Her eyes were shut, and she hadn't noticed. 'I *do* get it, though. When you're young and you don't know how reality works, when you don't know that there's no such things ghosts or goblins or flying saucers or whatever, the world outside can appear to be a dangerous, chaotic place. Pallid spectres on the landing, waiting to jump out and bite you on your way to the toilet. Or maybe a UFO has landed in the back garden, and there's an alien with large black expressionless eyes at the foot of the stairs intent on beaming you up to the mothership and off to Zeta Reticuli.'

'*Yes*! And the worst of it is that I imagined I could accidentally bring these horrors into existence by pure force of will, that they'd jump off the page and into the real world if I simply thought about them too hard – which is very difficult not to do. The human mind – *my* mind – and its powers of imagination.'

'Then you grow up, leave school, go to college, get a job and realise the world doesn't work like that.'

Mia rolled over so her back was towards him. 'Have you ever seen a ghost? Something you couldn't explain?'

Isaac shifted down into the covers, set the book on his chest and folded his arms across it. 'Maybe. If I was given to such things ... For instance—' He paused.

'For instance?'

'I was, I don't know, seven or eight, maybe. The family was staying in this holiday flat in Cirencester. A week out of London, a week of walks in the rain around flooded car parks and closed National Trust castles. I was sharing the attic room with James—'

'Your brother?'

'My real brother. James had the top bunk. I had the bottom. I'm lying there, and in the half light I suddenly see this wolf by the door, mouth open, silent, unmoving. I immediately sit straight up, and, it being a bunk bed and all, I catch my hair on the springs. 'I—*saaaac*!', says James, and turns on the light. And it's just my dressing gown. Hanging on a hook on the back of the door.'

'No wolf.'

'Only an overactive imagination.'

'But ... do wolves wear dressing gowns?' Mia spun a finger.

'You know, if they need to use the toilet in the middle of the night, perhaps?'

'*Ha*. Course they do. Confuses the pallid spectres I told you about earlier. *Anyway*. Pass my glasses. Chapter one, coming up.'

Isaac opened the book and turned to the first page.

> *Welcome, children, to the Manor*
> *Do not be afraid;*
> *We'll help you to negotiate*
> *Life's grand masquerade!*

Isaac paused to look over at Mia. Her expression was hard to decipher.

> *Preparation for your station—*
> *King or slave or knave;*
> *'Fore graduation comes around you'll*
> *Learn how to behave!*

The whole book appeared to be written in this fashion, four or five verses to a page.

Twenty minutes later Isaac laid the open book down on the blanket beside him. 'I'm beginning to understand why this story freaked you out. It isn't what I expected. This is for *kids*? The language is—'

'Baroque.'

'Any PTSD flashbacks?'

'No ... But it's ... curious, don't you think? When was it written?'

Isaac flipped back to the colophon. 'Printed in Munich. Translated from the Scandinavian, it says here. No date.' Inserting a thumb to act as a bookmark, he turned to the cover. 'It looks, I don't know – 1880? Earlier, judging by the style? Your parents were happy to let you read this kind of stuff?'

'My parents didn't know I was reading this kind of stuff because I read it alone, at night. I felt guilty about, uh, borrowing it without permission, remember. And if they *had* – they'd probably just be happy I was reading. They weren't about to regulate my intake.'

2

THE FOLLOWING night Isaac read Mia chapter two. He suspected the elusive P. K. Meek had intended it to be read aloud; it had a cadence, a rhythm – a bit like an incantation.

> ***Elias studied Math and Law,***
> ***Egregores and Art;***
> ***Tomas, he liked Alchemy, and***
> ***Napoleon Bonaparte.***

The story, so far: our hero, young Tomas, was a wan child who lived with his brother, Elias, his older sister Thea, a small cast of other children and a menagerie of talking dogs, cats and monkeys. They all wore the same outfit, a cross between a nightgown and a school uniform with a peaked cap. They were looked after by a governess – Isaac assumed she was a governess, but their exact relationship didn't seem to be specified. Schoolteacher, aunt? It might have been obvious enough back in 1880 that P. K. Meek didn't feel it was necessary to elucidate. Did they live in a castle? An orphanage? A boarding school? Times, they have a habit of changing, and things that might once have seemed unworthy of explanation can eventually become utterly opaque.

Every dozen or so pages an illustration printed on shinier paper had been tipped in. These were in black and white, finely etched, and resembled a cross between the epic biblical fantasies of Gustav Doré and the domestic peculiarities of Edward Gorey. 'A Gorydoré', Mia suggested.

Isaac lifted the book a fraction so that she could see the drawing placed opposite the title page. She lifted her head from his forearm and briefly glanced over, but didn't seem to want to examine it more closely. 'Those illustrations. They sort of repelled and seduced me in equal measure. That scritchy, scratchy mess o' lines, precise but indistinct at the same time. Like *anything* could be in there. A kind of nightmare Rorschach test. *Brrrr*.'

Isaac turned the book back towards him. She had a point. It was sometimes hard to work out if the action, whatever it was, was taking place indoors or outdoors – there might be tall windows, an ornate chandelier, high baroque ceilings; but then there were also trees and animals, streams crossed by arched stone bridges. Doors would open into brightly lit desert landscapes, or a bathroom with fish swimming through transparent pipework, or a long corridor hung with the mounted heads of mythical beasts – or they may have been old pupils, or inmates – the text didn't exactly make it clear.

All this weirdness was overseen by the Grande Dame, who appeared to be a cross between a schoolmistress and a warden – it did all depend on what kind of establishment Tomas might be in. The Grande Dame was an imposing woman with a tall wig in which small ships and mermaids frolicked.

> *Tomas worked alone at night,*
> *His knowledge to improve;*
> *A tulpa was his faithful aide*
> *Though Thea disapproved.*

'Tulpa? I don't remember a tulpa.' Mia's voice was a distracted mumble, hovering on the edge of sleep.

'Well, it definitely says "tulpa" here. One more verse, then we'll call it quits for tonight.'

> *'Don't conjure what you can't control!'*
> *She pled with him to quit.*
> *But Tomas, now by work consumed,*
> *Thought he could contain it.*

Mia was now snoring in a light, ladylike fashion beside him. He glanced at the dressing gown hanging on the back of the door, but it was just a regular dressing gown.

3

CHAPTER THREE (how many chapters were there? Deciding not to flip forward and spoil the story did have its downsides) was illustrated by the scene which also featured on the cover. The publisher had obviously decided that this was a good, strong image to place up front, and it certainly held the attention. There was Tomas, small and pale, and behind him that looming shape. Isaac flipped to the cover and back again to compare the two images.

> *A gloaming shape behind him rose*
> *As Tomas cast in vain.*
> *His wayward tulpa's new abode?*
> *Elias was his name.*

Ah – this was the origin of the Other Brother Mia remembered.

'Hang on a moment. My memory is— I don't recall this part very clearly. It seems – *different*.'

'Different?'

Mia did not respond.

Other than Tomas, the cast didn't seem to be too concerned

about this new development. In fact they acted as if they were completely unaware of it. Issac silently reread the previous few stanzas in case he'd missed something, but there was no further explanation.

Elias, Thea, and a talking cat in a waistcoat called Captain Tabby were now discussing where they might find a fourth for a game of bridge. The Grande Dame was not the kind to indulge such pastimes, so there was a certain amount of subterfuge involved. Tomas suggested that they ask the Other Brother, as long as he promised not to cheat.

Mia turned her head up to Isaac. Her soft, tired voice sounded like it was coming from a world away. 'Bridge? It was Pachisi.'

'It says bridge here.'

Mia was silent for a moment. Isaac wondered if she'd fallen asleep. 'Definitely Pachisi.' Her voice was barely a whisper, and her eyes were shut.

Isaac marked their place with the Otter Books receipt and, trying not to disturb her, put the book on the bedside table and turned out the light.

4

CHAPTER FOUR revolved around an attempt to escape by hiding in a laundry van. Their ruse was quickly rumbled – an illustration of Tomas with a pair of pantaloons on his head provided the light relief.

In with the socks! In with the pants!
Through those gates we'll ride;
If fortune is our friend today
I'll see you on the other side!

'This institution – it's not a boarding school, is it? I'm beginning to think it could be a *sanatorium*—'

Mia was adamant. 'It's a school. *Definitely* a school. There's that bit near the beginning about the open day, and Tomas is dropped off by his mother who drives a Bentley. When I was nine, I thought "Bentley" was a curious name for a car – as if it's been in some kind of accident, and is all bent up.'

'I don't recall reading that.'

'I must have fallen asleep. Go back.'

Isaac flipped back a few pages, forward again, then back to the start. 'No Bentley.'

Mia sat up. She was now fully awake. 'That's *not* what happens. That's not what I remember. You've been making stuff up, haven't you?'

'Me? No! Why would I do that?'

'I don't know. To mess with me.'

'Mia, why would I—'

'Fuck you, Isaac Livingstone.'

'I am not messing with you! Honestly, look. Read it yourself!'

Mia took the book and read, running her finger down each short page of text in turn. She could feel the impression of metal type on wove paper: old books, they were imbued with the physicality of their manufacture. They were made of *stuff*, unlike the fleeting text on the ash-grey screen of her Kindle. She imagined that, through her finger, it might be possible to trace a connection right back to the press and the bindery, and through them to the author themselves – and perhaps divine their intent.

Isaac was right. There was no mention of a Bentley, or of Tomas' mother. Mia held the cover closer to the bedside lamp. 'Maybe I've got it all wrong. Maybe I'm misremembering, and it was a different book. But that cover. I remember—

'P. K. Meek. Did they write anything else?'

Isaac reached over for his smartphone and began poking and scrolling. 'No copies on AbeBooks.' A few more jabs at the screen. 'In fact, no mention of *The Other Brother* anywhere. Or of our P. K. Meek, other than a chiropractor in Florida. That might not mean anything, though – there must be thousands of forgotten authors whose legacy is crated up in storage, or sitting, unread and unremembered, on the shelves of obscure second-hand bookshops.'

'Well, I didn't just imagine it all. We have a copy right here.' She rapped the book across Isaac's forehead. 'See? It definitely exists.'

Mia looked again at the cover, and the old-fashioned illustration that had evoked so many mixed emotions in her young mind. It was a kind of time travel – after decades of unremarkable unmysterious adulthood the vivid memory of that childhood dislocation began to come back to her: the feeling that the familiar world was built on fragile foundations, and that they could be so easily unthought by careless minds. All those ominous ideas began to well up inside her like a buried cardboard box that threatened to disinter its dark secrets.

5

THE FOLLOWING evening proved to be a short hiatus in their reading schedule. Isaac was out late with associates from the office; there had been some unexpected shakeup in upper management, and though the details were unclear, he had been assured he was meeting all his targets. Of *course* he met all his targets; he was a conscientious rep. Real attention to detail. If was given a job to do, he'd see it through till the end.

He wondered if Mia might have read ahead without him, but

when he slid into bed around 1.30am he could see that the bookmark was exactly where he'd left it.

Mia turned over in her sleep as he adjusted his pillow. Her voice was plaintive, as if it was coming from somewhere far away: 'No, no, you can't take me away ... I have *protection*. I have a special something, waiting for you here if you try ...'

'Mia? You OK, Mia?'

Her cheek twitched and she exhaled abruptly. 'Mmm, s'ok. They can't get me ... I'm ok ...' She turned onto her back. She was plainly asleep, but Isaac could see her eyes darting back and forth behind her lids.

They resumed the following night. Isaac guessed chapter five could be the penultimate chapter; they were well past the halfway mark.

Elias – or Tomas's Other Brother – had assumed the role of leader, though his sister did not seem entirely happy with this arrangement. Perhaps she knew something was amiss too, though she refused to share her suspicions with Tomas. Regardless, The Other Brother had *plans*.

A few days after their laundry van escapade had been foiled, our heroes were contemplating scaling the wall at the bottom of the Bone Orchard.

A handhold here, foothold there
Then reach up for that coping~
Pull yourself up to the top
From here, we are eloping!

'No. This is *wrong*. They don't try and escape – term ends, and Tomas's parents come to collect him. There's a big graduation ceremony, and he's awarded a first in something like croquet, or jousting, I forget what, exactly. The Other Brother opts to stay behind now Tomas has graduated to the real, adult world; it's time to say farewell to your imaginary friends. A metaphor for letting go of childish things, I guess.'

Isaac was silent for a moment. 'That's not what—'

'Isaac, *honestly* – if this is all some kind of elaborate practical joke, well done, I get it, good for you, pat on the back—'

'I can only read you what it says right here.'

'You've pasted in new pages—'

Isaac snorted. 'What? No, of *course* I haven't. How would I even do such a thing? Look – the paper, the printing – how could I create a new version of a book I didn't even know *existed* until you found it last week?'

Mia gave him an uncompromising stare from under a lowered brow, then snatched the book from his hands. 'Enough, Isaac. I *remember what happens*. This story has stayed with me for over twenty five years.'

She reread the page Isaac had just read aloud. She turned back a couple of pages, then read it again, more carefully, as if creeping up on the passage in question would disabuse it of its obvious chicanery and make it conform to her expectations.

It was exactly as Isaac had read it aloud. Not a word was different.

She closed the book, looked at the spine. 'This is so *freaky*.'

'Another edition?'

'No, this is definitely the version I had. I remember the colour, the size. I remember that illustration. It's not the kind of image you'd easily forget. But that's *not* what happened in my copy. I'm absolutely certain of it.'

'Maybe this is an uncorrected proof, or something.'

'Authors correct the odd typo, they don't rewrite the entire story.'

'You're absolutely sure you're not mistaken?'

'Are you suggesting I'm losing it? That I'm making all this up?'

'No … I— Listen, Mia, I don't know *what* to think.'

'You don't believe me, do you?'

There was a long pause punctuated only by the squeal of a distant train. When Isaac eventually spoke, his voice had a frayed, unfamiliar edge to it. 'So – you want to find out how it ends?'

6

MIA WRIGGLED down and pulled the blankets up under her nose so just her eyes were visible, dark but for small pinpoint reflections from the streetlight outside. 'Go on. Read it to me. But let me *see*. Let me follow along.'

Isaac turned the page to reveal another illustration tipped in on a separate sheet. Standing alone on the steps of the institution, flanked by tall shrubs sculpted into rearing unicorns, were Tomas, Thea, Captain Tabby and Elias. Behind the four of them was the black shape with smudges for eyes and that long curling mouth that went right around its head like a thin white ribbon.

Was it how she remembered?

What *did* she remember?

At home, in her childhood bedroom, surrounded by her stuffed rabbits and picturebooks and sketchpads and school holiday souvenirs, she had felt safe. Her personal inner sanctum was an impregnable space where she could pull up a metaphorical drawbridge and the stresses and challenges of the real world, of how to negotiate friendships, algebra homework and sports days, couldn't reach her. The bad things all happened somewhere else; horrors, real or imaginary, could not find her here.

Then she'd encountered this book.

The intervening years collapsed like a wet newspaper and she was that young girl again, the one who had been driven to bury it, to neuter its power to disturb her.

What if that personal haven *could* been breached by someone familiar, someone close to you, someone who wasn't who or what you thought they were?

What if the bottom *could* suddenly drop out of your whole world, and there was absolutely nothing you could do about it except scream the whole way down?

But she remembered what happened next. In *her* version that is. In the *real* version.

Tomas was a bright and resourceful child. He knew what was at stake. If the Other Brother had taken up residence inside Elias, if he was, for all intents and purposes, now indistinguishable from Elias, that was his weakness. Whereas the Other Brother may not have had a corporeal form that could be hurt, Elias *did* – and as Elias was not Elias any more, as he had already been taken away to who knows where he could not be hurt any more than he had already been hurt.

Tomas was not usually permitted to roam the kitchens, but the Grand Dame had acquiesced to his insistent request that he help out, at least with the washing of the dishes and the mopping of the floors. The knife from the pantry would not be missed, of that he was certain. There were so many of them, in all sizes, hanging from that long rack above the stove. He only needed the one.

> *One for butter, one for bread,*
> *One for peeling fruit;*
> *One for carving, then you're–*

Mia let her arm drop from the side of the bed where she was lying. She walked the tips of her fingers across the floorboards, finding the item she'd sequestered there the night before.

LATER, AFTER she'd wiped the kitchen knife clean on his pillow, she picked the book up from the floor where it had fallen.

There, on the cover, the dark indistinct apparition still smiled its indecipherable smile. She wrapped Isaac in the blanket, placing *The Other Brother* under the last layer like a talismanic Egyptian guide to the afterlife, then threaded a belt around the bundle, pulled it tight, and began dragging him towards the door, the stairs, and the back garden.

Tonight she'd need more than a spoon.

ABOUT THE AUTHOR

RIAN HUGHES is a graphic designer, illustrator, comic artist, writer and typographer who has worked extensively for the British and American advertising, music and comic book industries.

He has written and drawn comics for *2000AD*, Vertigo and *Batman: Black and White*, and designed hundreds of logos for DC Comics, Marvel and other companies, including *Batman*, the *X-Men*, *Superman*, *James Bond* and *The Avengers*. He has produced Hawaiian shirts, ranges for Swatch, record sleeves for Ultravox, and designed many typefaces which are available through his foundry, Device Fonts.

His illustrations have appeared in magazines in the UK, US and Japan, and a retrospective monograph collecting his work, *Art, Commercial*, was published in 2001. His comic strips have been collected in *Yesterday's Tomorrows* and *Tales from Beyond Science*, and his burlesque portraits in *Soho Dives, Soho Divas. Logo a Gogo* collects all his logo designs for the comic-book world and beyond.

His first novel, *XX*, was published by Picador in 2020, which he describes as a 'novel, graphic'. This was followed by *The Black Locomotive* in 2021. His third novel, *The Absence* is currently limping towards completion.

STAY IN TOUCH

LINDY RYAN

'I just think I should be the one to plan the party,' says Dear, once they're all seated around the four-top in the old woman's senior living kitchenette, the same as every Thursday evening. 'It is *my* funeral, for Pete's sake.'

And your money, Bernice might add, if it weren't so crass. After all, everyone knows the funeral business is a racket. What kind of service charges people to die, anyway? But someone's got to pay for the flowers, the casket, the Kleenex. Might as well take it out of the deceased's bank account. It's not like they'll need the cash.

Not that there's much left in Dear's accounts. The medical bills have seen to that. *If you think livin' is expensive*, the old woman has become fond of saying, *just wait 'til you try dyin'*.

Bernice tightens her lips. 'Planning your own funeral is morbid, Dear,' she says.

'And *strange*,' adds Carol, whose dusty linguistics degree would argue the difference.

The flick of Dear's wrist is barely enough to clang the bracelets stacked up her forearm—the best she can do, given her condition, but chemo does that. 'I'm the guest of honour, aren't I?' she says, and the heart-shaped plank shudders beside the wooden board centred on the lace tablecloth. 'I reckon I should have a say.'

Nell hoists a silver pie server over the glass dish squared atop the wooden board. 'But Dear, honey,' she says, 'it's a *funeral*—'

'*Your* funeral,' Carol cuts in.

'And there's nothing *fun* about plannin' that,' Nell finishes, slicing through pie crust. The dish is from Nell's China hutch, but the pie is from the Market Basket frozen foods aisle. Amongst its many amenities, Twilight Gardens Senior Living Community boasts a world-class dining room and a five-star kitchen, though the best one can hope for in their individual apartment is a mini fridge and a microwave. But who among them has the energy to bake these days anyway? These days, store bought is every bit as good as homemade.

Dear shrugs mink-stole shoulders while Nell passes plates around the table. 'That's precisely why I should be the one to do it: I'm gonna put the *fun* back in *funeral*,' she says, and the rap of her bejewelled knuckles on the lace tablecloth makes the little plank jump again. 'Make sure everyone has a good time.'

Bernice bristles. Like her diagnosis, the old woman's typically morbid Southern sense of gallows humour has gone from bad to worse—a shade too dark, even to Bernice's tastes, which is saying something, all things considered. 'Dear, nothing about your funeral is going to be *a good time*,' she says flatly.

Carol sniffs. 'It'll be just *awful*.'

'I don't know how I'll be able to bear it,' says Nell, forking into a fat slice of cherry crumble.

Dear sits stoic behind her bifocals, and the little plank jiggles again. 'You'll live,' she tells them, and all three women shiver despite the balmy heat of the old woman's apartment. Seventy-six degrees is enough to help ward off a dying woman's chills, but not her friends' sense of propriety. Then again, Dear is the only one wearing her best furs along with every piece of jewellery she owns.

Not that she can take any of it with her, Bernice thinks, so what's the harm? Every bit and bauble will soon be doled out to friends and relatives. The pie will only hold so long, and the night will soon end, so the old woman might as well enjoy them while she can.

Even so.

'Nobody is planning their own funeral, Miss Haversham,' she tells the bundle of jewels and furs on the other side of the small table.

Dear hitches an eyebrow and the little plank jiggles. 'I've got a knack for plannin' these sorts of things,' she says. 'Always have, you know.'

Heat prickles behind Bernice's eyes, but she blinks it back, because of course they know. The four of them have been friends ever since they all moved onto Comstock Road, their kids still in diapers and their spouses still above ground. From birthday potlucks to block parties, Mother's Day bruncheons to Fourth of July barbeques, nearly every neighbourhood event for the past forty-odd years has been planned by Dear. Not that Bernice has been keeping count, but however many years they've been friends, it's since well before they sold their three-beds, two-baths and moved en masse into Twilight Gardens.

And just what else were we supposed to do? Bernice would like to know. Their partners were gone, and their kids were grown, and really, who had any use for all that empty space? Besides, none of them could imagine Comstock Road without Dear—not that they can imagine a Dear-less Twilight Gardens either. At seventy-two, the old woman has beat the odds, but sooner or later they all give up the ghost, and it's almost Dear's time.

'And don't forget, girls,' she says, stabbing a single, ring-stacked digit toward the kitchenette ceiling, and Carol sniffs again when the little plank jumps on the lace tablecloth. 'This whole thing was my idea to start with.'

Sugary pie guts jiggle on the prongs of Nell's fork when she stabs it in Dear's direction. 'Plannin' a weekly get-together and plannin' your own funeral are two *very* different things,' she says.

The old woman shrugs under layers of jewels and fur. 'Well, it's not like I can leave the important details to you three old fuddy-duddies,' she says. 'This one won't be able to quit cryin'—' She points first at Carol, still sniffing into her teacup, and then to Nell, already halfway through her second slice of pie. 'And this one will be too busy eatin' her feelings.'

'And me?' Bernice is dying to know.

Dear peers down her nose at the wooden board under the pie dish, then up at the kitchenette's popcorn ceiling. 'Well, I did say I want to put the *fun* back in funeral, didn't I?'

If the old woman's cancer hadn't already killed her, Bernice might strangle Dear with her silly own mink. She fusses now, but who had Dear called when she needed a ride to her beauty salon appointment, her doctor, her dry cleaner? Bernice might be an old fuddy-duddy, but she's the only old fuddy-duddy seated at the table who still drives her own car.

Dear goes through the trouble to stick out her tongue at Bernice, and Bernice puckers. It's always been impossible, arguing with Dear. Just because this is the last time doesn't make it any easier.

Carol sniffs again. 'Let's not talk about this anymore. It's too sad.'

'You're tellin' me,' says Dear. 'I'm the one who's dead, remember?'

'We are supposed to be scarin' each other silly with spooky stories,' Nell reminds Dear. 'Not makin' poor Carol cry.'

'Unless you've forgotten what it is we do every Thursday evening,' adds Bernice, though to be totally fair, Carol has always been something of a cream puff.

Dear rolls her eyes. 'You three wouldn't even be here talkin' to ghosts if it weren't for me,' she says, which is true enough. When, years ago, the woman had suggested they spend their Thursday evenings telling each other ghost stories, Bernice couldn't imagine what four aging suburban housewives knew about spooks and spirits. They'd stuck with it, and now here they were, and of course it had all been Dear's idea, because who else but Dear would suggest they abandon book club and girls' night and dabble instead with communing with the dead.

'Well it's downright depressin',' says Nell. 'The four of us, sittin' around the table at half past midnight, talkin' about each other's funerals.' She fidgets with the wooden board on the lace tablecloth, careful not to touch the little dancing plank. 'Why, we're nothin' but a bunch of spooky old bats!'

Dear lifts her chin, and the dim kitchenette light catches the gemstones in her earrings. 'I prefer "glamorous ghoul,"' she says, and a sly grin spreads over her rouged lips. Red creeps outside the lines, settling into the wrinkles around her mouth, but the old woman's eyeliner is as straight as always, her eyes just as bright. 'Has a better ring to it, don't you think?'

If Bernice's lips pull any flatter, they'll be nothing but a line. 'More like dramatic banshee,' she mutters.

'I don't want to be a bat *or* a ghoul,' whimpers Carol, dabbing at her eyes with a crumpled tissue. 'Why can't we just be normal? Normal old women don't sit around planning each other's funerals.'

'Normal old women bore themselves to death.' The tablecloth stirs when Dear waves her hand as if swatting away an invisible fly. 'Besides, I've got to do something to keep this little group of ours from turning into…' She pauses for dramatic effect, narrowing her eyes, and the heart-shaped plank on the table spins accusingly in Bernice's direction. 'A knitting circle?'

Bernice folds her arms over her chest. 'I'll have you know I'm very good at knitting,' she says. 'And there's nothing wrong with a little peace and quiet every now and then.'

'Peace and quiet is a slow death,' says Dear. 'Mark my words, once I'm gone, you three will be sittin' around this table playin' bridge and eatin' Jell-O moulds within six months.'

'Now that's uncalled for,' says Nell, on her third slice of cherry pie, clearly scandalised.

'That's why I say we go out kickin' and screamin',' says Dear. Her rings disappear into her nest of skirts, then reappear with a sheet of crumpled stationery that she smooths open on the tabletop. 'I've taken the liberty of jotting down some ideas for my farewell party.'

'Oh good,' says Bernice. 'You've put together a list of demands.'

Dear lifts her chin, unaffected. 'I want balloons, not flowers,' she says, 'I've got allergies.'

'Allergies?' Nell pauses mid-bite. 'But Dear, honey, you're—'

'And I want music, preferably a live band,' the old woman goes on. 'People are more likely to get up and dance if there's a real band.'

'Sure,' says Bernice, because funeral services are well-known performance venues. That will be a fun request, she thinks. What kind of band would jump at the change to play at an old woman's funeral, anyway? Probably not the sort often invited to Twilight Gardens.

'And I want food at the reception.' The little plank spins on the table as the old woman makes her way down her list. 'Good, home-cooked Southern food, none of that cafeteria slop served in those cheap aluminum trays—and nothin' frozen.' Dear wrinkles her nose at the half-eaten cherry pie in the dish atop the wooden board. 'Pimento cheese sandwiches, dumplings, creamed corn…'

'Is this a funeral you're planning or a picnic?' Bernice has to know.

'Save your energy for the banana pudding,' snaps Dear, who still isn't finished. 'And don't forget extra Nilla Wafers—and don't skimp with the generic, either. Get the brand name.' A cough cracks open the old woman's voice, and a storm surges through her body like static, the heart-shaped plank skittering across the lace tablecloth. Despite her hearty appetite, Dear has always been a petite woman. Now there's so little of her left that it's possible to believe she might blow herself to pieces before she's finished reading off her list.

Nell dabs at the corners of her eyes as Dear collects herself. Carol sniffs harder, and even Bernice feels a tingle in her nose. All this talk about funerals and balloons and live music and home cooking would be outrageously silly, really, if it weren't so horribly, horribly sad. But with every breath, the sands in Dear's hourglass are trickling low, and as the old woman herself said, she's always been the one with the knack for party-planning.

And she *is* the guest of honour.

'We'll be sure to get the real thing,' says Carol, about the Nilla Wafers, with another sniff.

Dear waggles her pencilled-on eyebrows, primping her freshly permed curls. 'And leave my casket open, so I can see who shows up,' she says. 'In case I feel like hauntin' someone later.'

Never one to be jilted, Dear. 'Anything else?' says Bernice.

'Just one thing,' Dear says as she folds her paper back into her skirt folds. 'I want the three of you to give my eulogy.'

Nell nearly chokes on a bite of cherry crumble and Carol sniffs bubbles into her teacup. Bernice blanches. *I'd rather die*, she doesn't say, but nothing scares the hell out of Bernice like public speaking.

'The three of us?' says Nell, palm to her heart as her eyes slide to Carol, then to Bernice. 'But, Dear, honey—why us?'

'Surely you can find *someone* who has something nice to say about you?' says Bernice.

Dear fiddles with her jewels. 'Why not? We get together every week to tell each other stories.' She shrugs again, growing fainter still. 'You three know all my best hits.'

'Yes, but Dear, telling each other scary stories once a week is not even close to the same thing as givin' your eulogy,' says Nell.

'Sure, it is.' Dear primps her mink collar, her double-looped pearls. 'Just tell your best stories about me.' She twists the rings over the knots in her fingers to make sure they catch the light, and pets her furs. 'And make 'em scary,' she says. 'The scarier, the better.'

'Scary stories?' says Carol. 'But aren't you already scared enough?'

'I've had a long time to get used to the idea of dyin'.' Dear manages a weak smile, and Bernice can tell the old woman is fading now, the heart-shaped plank growing still on the lace. 'Only thing I'm scared of now is missin' you girls every Thursday night,' she says.

Bernice reaches for her friend's hand, but her palm stops on the wooden board at the table's centre. The cancer has stolen the old woman's remaining years, but it's taken time away from all of them. It's hard now to remember a time before Dear, and nothing will be the same without her.

Nell lays her hand atop Bernice's. 'Every Thursday night,' she says, and squeezes.

'And all the other times, too,' says Carol, joining the pile.

'We've had some good times, haven't we, girls?' says Dear, so weak now that the planchette barely shivers on the lace. She nods at the wooden board under the glass pie dish, mostly empty now, its contents stuffed inside Nell. 'Promise me you'll stay in touch after I'm gone?'

Of course we will, Bernice would say, but the old woman at the other end of the table is gone before the words leave her mouth. The planchette lies still on the lace tablecloth, its tip pointed toward the bottom corner of the wooden board on the kitchenette's small four-top.

Goodbye, says Dear, and all that's left of the old woman now is the sweet scent of her perfume, and the last glimmers of her jewels in the dim kitchenette light.

'Well,' says Nell, 'what do we do now?'

Bernice licks her lips. She hands off the pie dish, gathers up the spirit board and the planchette, and looks toward the senior living apartment's small bedroom, at the small form draped in furs resting atop the small bed in the centre of the room. 'Well girls,' she says, 'it sounds like we have a party to plan.'

ABOUT THE AUTHOR

LINDY RYAN is an award-winning author, anthologist, and short-film director. She also writes sweet, seasonal romance under the pseudonym Lindy Miller, with several projects having been adapted for screen.

Ryan is the current author-in residence at *Rue Morgue*, and regularly contributes articles to outlets including *BookTrib, Crime reads*, and more. Declared a 'champion of women's voices in horror' by *Shelf Awareness*, Ryan was named a *Publishers Weekly* Star Watch Honoree in 2020, and named one of horror's most masterful anthology creators in 2022. She has previously served on the Board of Directors for the Independent Book Publishers Association (IBPA).

She is an award-winning professor at Rutgers University, and has published several academic texts. Prior to her career in academia, Ryan was the co-founder of Radiant Advisors, a business intelligence research and advisory firm, where - as research director and then chief operations officer – she led the company's research and data enablement practice for clients including 21st Century Fox Films, Warner Bros., and Disney.

Born and raised in Southeast Texas, Ryan currently resides on the East Coast.

MR PERFECT

SUSI HOLLIDAY

It started with the grooming.

No, not that creepy paedo stuff. Actual grooming. Choosing my clothes. Personal hygiene. New deodorant. An eyebrow pluck and shape. Nose hair removal.

She liked to remove in-growing hairs on my neck with tweezers, relishing it all just a bit too much, brandishing the little hair with the pus-smeared root attached, ignoring my small yelps of pain. *Man up*, she'd whisper in my ear. That breathy little giggle she did. She lanced a boil once. Sharp needle sterilised with a lighter, bowl of fresh hot facecloths for before and after. That one hurt like fuck but there was relief at the end.

Then she started cutting my hair.

I was fine with it at first. I'd never been much into that stuff and it was nice to have someone looking after me. She was all about the looks and the scents and the outward appearance apparently bringing inner calm. It's not vanity, she said. It's personal wellbeing. You smell *divine.* See how much better you feel when you look good and people notice you?

She was right about that. And I guess I did want to feel better about myself.

Before I met her, I was invisible. People would barge past me on the street, looking cross and swearing as if I was the one who wasn't looking where I was going. I could stand at the bar for hours trying to get served. I had the wrong face or something.

But *she* saw me.

When she came up beside me, told the barman to serve me next, and actually smiled … I was sure she'd mistaken me for someone else. I looked behind me when she spoke. Hi! Big white teeth, two perfect rows. I'm talking to you, silly. I felt the heat rise in my cheeks. Managed to order a pint of Carlsberg for me and then asked her what she wanted. She grinned. That's so kind, she said. Asked the barman for a Bacardi and soda with a slice of fresh lime and lots of ice. Then she took my elbow and led me out away from the crowded bar area to a high table in the corner. Asked me if I wanted to join her.

I assumed it was a prank. Kept looking around to see which of my stupid work colleagues had set me up. They were probably filming it so they could pass it around the department WhatsApp group that no one had added me to. They all think I'm a weirdo. I don't dress in their cheap office fashion clothes. Pointy shoes. Skinny trousers and too-tight jumpers, little rolls of belly hanging over the waistband. I've had these navy cords for fifteen years but I wash them carefully and they've lasted me well.

I wasn't always like this. When you lose everything, you stop caring about the superficial bullshit that carries on around you, but the problem with shutting down is that you become insular and then it's really hard to find a way back out. I do believe that if anyone at work had asked me why I was so fucking weird instead of just whispering it behind my back when I was making my own cup of tea in the kitchen, sitting on my own to eat my own packet of Bourbon creams – I would have told them.

I had a wife, I would say. I had a child.

They died.

Anyway. I didn't tell her this. I don't talk about it, but I think she knew that I was a husk. I didn't question why she wanted to talk to me, I just savoured the moment of a good-looking woman sitting and having a drink with me. I tried to listen to everything she was saying, despite all the eyes on me – the little nudges – the whispers.

What the fuck is she doing with him?

Is this care in the community?

You have the most incredible eyes, she was saying, and I snapped back into the moment with her. Because let's face it, it was only going to be a moment.

And your hair is such a gorgeous shade of brown. Those little flecks of auburn look like you've had expensive highlights.

I took a sip of my pint and tried hard to supress a smile. Highlights? Me? Even before, I was very much a short back and sides, wash with the cheapest shampoo kind of guy.

Do you want to come home with me? A bead of condensation slid down her glass. She licked her lips. Bright and shiny as a red apple.

Why?

You're not that naïve, she said.

By the way, when I said good-looking I actually meant stunning. Eyes the colour of fresh moss. Pin-straight hair. Raven black you might say. Her skin was like fresh milk. She wore a tight silver dress that hugged her in all the right places. As she got up from her seat, the slowly revolving disco ball lighting bounced off her curves and gave her the look of some sort of ethereal being.

Well, I thought, prank it might be, but I'm going to savour this moment while it lasts.

It's been four months.

It wasn't a prank.

I've barely left her side since I met her.

Work weren't very happy when I emailed to say I wasn't coming back, but I think they were just going through the motions. I'm sure they were secretly relieved to see the back of me. I've still got my house. It was all paid for with life insurance after the accident, and I pay all the bills by direct debit. There was no food in the fridge to go off. No one sends me any mail. It was surprisingly easy to stay with her in her trendy loft apartment and forget that I even had another life before.

That's why I was happy enough to go along with all her suggestions. It was just for us, she said. It's not like I wanted to go anywhere. See anyone. It's not like it hurt that much.

Not in the beginning.

She bought this stuff that she said would sort out my wonky teeth. I was mildly alarmed at that. I had no idea I had wonky teeth. I'd stopped bothering with the dentist years ago, but I cleaned and flossed, and my gums were a healthy pink. No blood. No discolouration of the enamel.

Oh I know, she said. But they're just a bit last century, you know? We go for a more uniform look now. A whiter white. Like mine. She grinned that grin, and just for a moment her mouth made me think of the rows of white goods in an electrical store.

But I let her do it anyway. Of course I did. She gave me something to numb the pain and put headphones on me, playing an old album by some grungy rock band called Alice in Chains. Really fucking loud. Something about a sick man, sick man, sick man.

It was hard to eat after that. I think she shaved too much off the bottom row, and it meant when I bit together, it was all sort of unaligned. Made my jaw ache. Don't worry, she said. I'll make you nice soups. They were nice, to be fair. I loved her broccoli and blue cheese one. I watched her eating chunks of sourdough with hers and felt a little envious, but she would smile at me with those perfect teeth and then she'd do stuff to me with those perfect lips, and food didn't seem that important anymore.

Eventually, the pain in my jaw got worse. Infected, she said. She gave me a strong vodka cocktail then strapped me to a bed before removing my teeth with plyers. The headphones again, that song again. I never asked her why she kept playing it to me. She said she'd ordered me some clip-in dentures from this place online.

I didn't eat much at all after that. She mostly kept me strapped to the bed so she could carry out other procedures. Did I say bed? It wasn't a bed.

It was an operating table.

I've been here seven months. She doesn't suck my cock anymore but she keeps me on a drip so I don't starve to death. The dentures arrived, but they didn't really fit and just made it worse than having no teeth at all. I don't talk to her much now. My voice sounds funny and she frowns when she hears it. I don't think she factored in the inability to talk properly without teeth. Schoolgirl error.

I have a lot of time to think, just lying here drifting in and out of consciousness. She puts other sounds on the headphones now, that sort of white noise calming waves stuff. Sometimes I miss the rock music, but it's hard to sleep with that on. I remember back to the first few weeks in her apartment where we had sex all the time and ate grapes in bed, and she got everything delivered so we didn't have to leave the place. I realise now that's when she was taking the deliveries of the operating table, the surgical equipment. I remember now that when I was just lying in the bed, relaxing, feeling content with the new turn that my life had taken, that she was at the other end of the room, watching YouTube videos of extreme surgery. She said she was hoping to go to uni and study medicine. She wanted to immerse herself. Most of the videos were plastic surgeons doing unethical procedures to vulnerable women. Sometimes she would mutter at the screen, asking why was it always women. What about the men?

Why were the men in charge of what everyone was supposed to look like?

I knew she was obsessed with her own appearance. I knew it was a disorder. But when your life is dead, and someone breathes life into it, sometimes it pays not to ask too many questions. I kept telling myself it would end soon. That she would get bored. Move on to someone new.

She gave me a facelift last week. It didn't hurt, because she'd managed to get hold of some proper anaesthetic, and some proper pain relief. She videoed herself doing it and showed me when I woke up. I have to say, she did a good job. Sliced the skin behind my ears neatly and pulled everything up and cut off the excess. I'm not sure all the nerves and whatnot are completely back where they should be, as all I can feel is a strange pins and needles sensation. Apparently, it should wear off. She got me some more dentures to try and actually these ones are much better. I've tried talking again but the numbness in my face is making it difficult. My voice sounds kind of disembodied. She frowns when I speak, but she's removed the shackles and let me eat some proper food.

She lets me look in a full-length mirror, and I'm a bit shocked at first, and I think I must've cried because I could taste the salt on my lips but I couldn't feel the tears running down my cheeks. I'm much thinner now. But that's fine. I could have done with losing a few pounds. My hair is very nice. Kind of floppy at the front, short at the sides. It's shiny and nicely styled.

I smell good. *Divine*, in fact. She shows me the cologne and even I know it's an expensive one. I run my hands over my chest. I think it looks a bit sunken. She obviously thinks the same because she says she's ordered some implants and she's going to give me perfect pecs and washboard abs. I don't feel like me anymore. I need to tell you something, I say. My voice is strange. She frowns. Then she smiles. Puts a finger on my mouth. No need to speak, she says. We're nearly done. You're almost perfect.

Are you happy?

The others are happy.

I glance around at the photos of the other men. The photos that adorn every wall. Shiny floppy hair. Perfect faces. Perfect chests. Mouths fashioned into broad smiles. You can hardly see the stitches holding them in place. But where their eyes should be, there are dark holes, black thread in an oversized cross sewn over each one.

I hear my daughter's voice. *It's not a real smile unless it reaches your eyes, Daddy*. I closed my eyes for a moment, that's all it was. That's when the truck hit us. I died then, but somehow survived. Although it didn't feel like it. I want to die again. Properly this time. I'm ready.

What do you do with the eyes?

Shhh, she says.

ABOUT THE AUTHOR

SUSI (SJI) HOLLIDAY is a Scottish writer of dark fiction. She cut her teeth on flash fiction and short stories, and was shortlisted for the inaugural CWA Margery Allingham Prize in 2014.

She is the acclaimed author of the creepy and claustrophobic Banktoun trilogy (*Black Wood, Willow Walk* and *The Damselfly*), the festive serial killer thriller *The Deaths of December*, the supernatural mystery *The Lingering*, a psychological thriller set on the Trans-Siberian Express *(Violet)* and a horror novella *(Mr Sandman).* Her next two novels (*The Last Resort* and *Substitute)* contained a speculative science edge, and her post-pandemic thriller, *The Hike,* is another, like *Violet*, to feature travel adventures that go horribly wrong. Her tenth novel – *The Street* – took her back to her Scottish roots, with a brand-new housing development hiding sinister secrets. Her latest novel sees the return of Detectives Carmine & Greene in *The Party Season* – a seasonal tale of revenge.

Her short stories have been published in magazines, newspapers and anthologies. By day, she works as a clinical research statistician. Susi divides her time between London and Edinburgh. She loves travelling, long walks, '80s music, and trying to scare herself with horror movies.

BOW KNEE LAKE

TIM LEBBON

The man wakes slowly, stirring in his bed and stretching, shifting his limbs, cricking his back and neck. He grimaces, perhaps at the pain this causes him. He remains hugged beneath the blankets, and they lift and pulse as if the bed itself is alive. But it is only the man moving.

After a few minutes he peels the coverings aside and sits up on the edge of the bed. He sighs and slumps, as if these simple movements have taken a lot out of him. He reaches for a glass of water beside his bed and drinks from it, then pops some tablets from a blister pack and swallows them down.

The naked man is scarred all over. Some of the scars are ugly and ragged, but most of them seem more precise. Signs of surgeries, perhaps. The ring finger of his left hand bears a bright red wound along its length, and the harsh black specks of stitches. He examines his finger, turning his hand this way and that. He grunts in satisfaction, then stands.

He looks to be in his forties, but to begin with he moves like someone thirty years older. He's thin; malnourished-thin, not fit-thin. He still has all his hair and wears it long and unkempt. After performing a series of clearly regimented exercises he starts to move a little easier, dressing with slow, cautious motions.

He walks from his bedroom along the corridor to a small bathroom.

After performing his ablutions he goes to the kitchen and boils water for his morning tea, looking from the window as the kettle bubbles and hisses.

Seven minutes later he's outside. He walks barefoot across a lawn of long grass until he reaches a bench on the end of a wooden dock at the edge of the lake. By now he's moving almost like someone unhindered by pain. If he does experience discomfort he manages to barely show it, apart from a slight limp. He is smiling, enjoying the views, revelling in his surroundings, breathing in the early morning air. There's a soft mist on the lake but the sun is up now, and soon the haze will be burnt away.

Far out across the water a duck drifts down towards the surface, then seems to panic a little before changing its mind and flapping up and away.

The man drinks tea and watches the duck until it vanishes from view. He rubs his knee.

I arrived at the lakeside car park just before lunch. It had been a long drive of over three hours, and I was pleased to see a small toilet block at the car park's far end. Mine was the only car there—hardly a surprise, really—and I didn't bother locking the door before jogging towards the toilets. Bladder the size of a pea, my wife had sometimes said.

It was a warm, sunny day, and there was a subtle chemical smell on the air. It wasn't pleasant. Just another reason few people came to the lake any more. They said the place was an assault on the senses, and I knew I'd feel more of it soon.

The toilets were locked, the barred gates rusted in place. 'Fuck it,' I muttered. I doubted anyone had opened them in years. I looked around, dancing from foot to foot like a kid, then unzipped and huddled in close between the building and a bank of thick undergrowth. I sighed with relief as I pissed, drew a pattern on the brickwork, zipped up. There were wet-wipes in the car, part of the toolkit for my job. I figured I'd be needing them a lot today.

At first glance the lake was beautiful, its calm surface reflecting the startlingly blue summer sky with a mirror-like perfection, surrounding hills holding it safe from the world beyond, and trees growing here and there around its shore appeared mostly healthy. But a proportion of the evergreens were spotted with swathes of pale yellow needles, and among the spread of deciduous trees were a few ragged skeletons, denuded of leaves and life.

I breathed in deeply and smelled rot.

The beauty of the lake was misleading. It was polluted, poisonous, a place of lifelessness and decay. There were no water birds here, and the millpond surface indicated no insects, either. It was my third time visiting Bow Knee Lake in three years, and it was obviously getting worse and worse. It always saddened me, even though I was resigned to the inevitability of things. Once the rot had set in, it was almost impossible to reverse.

I opened the car boot and pulled on my protective clothing—bodysuit, boots, material helmet with breathing apparatus, tight gloves so that I was still dextrous enough to do what I needed to do. Then I grabbed the sample case and headed towards the lake. To begin with I'd felt pretty stupid dressed like an astronaut when I did these tests, but I'd quickly come to learn it was a necessity. Not in all cases—sometimes a river was dirty and polluted but not dangerous in small doses—but for a place like this, there was no such thing as over-cautious.

What happened to Mally had proved that. She was still my wife, but she wasn't really there anymore. Her mind had been changed, her flesh eaten away. I went to see her less and less often, because there was nothing of her left, and the guilt at these infrequent visits compounded my grief.

As I approached the lake I saw a man standing along the shore. There was a winding path that tourists had used to wander, cracked by weeds now and fully overgrown in places. He was following it towards me. He walked slowly, and I wondered if he was in pain.

'Morning!' he said, raising a hand to wave. Every movement was measured, considered.

'Good morning,' I said, words distorted by my mask. I pulled the hood back so that it hung down my back, and spoke again. 'Sorry. Morning.'

'Heard you the first time,' he said, smiling. 'Lovely morning.'

I looked up at the blue sky, fluffy with clouds. I supposed it was, though the lack of wildlife and the knowledge of the lake's taint stole any enjoyment from me.

'You testing the lake?'

'Yeah.' I held up the small sample case in my hand.

'Well, don't get too close. Water's bad.'

Hence me testing the fucking lake, I thought, but I smiled and nodded.

The man remained standing thirty metres away, staring. I had the distinct impression he was looking me up and down, though he wasn't smiling at my suit. His gaze settled on my legs.

'You live around here?' I asked.

He lifted a hand and pointed back over his shoulder with his thumb.

'Been here long?'

The man nodded. 'About seventeen years. Seen this place go from beautiful to…' He looked away from me and out across the water.

'You don't want to move?' I asked. I instantly berated myself. It was none of my business.

'Want's got nothing to do with it,' he said. He didn't elaborate, and I didn't push.

'It still looks beautiful,' I said, though I didn't really believe that at all. The lake was toxic, and it didn't even resemble the ghost of what it must have once been like. It was a corpse.

'So you people gonna try doing something about it?' he asked.

'I wish we could. I'm just here to take samples and keep track.'

'Keep track,' the man said, and for some reason he laughed. It sounded like gravel in a tin. 'What's your name?'

'Davey,' I said.

'Okay, Eighteen, I'm gonna finish my walk. I'll leave you to do your thing.'

I'm sure that's what he said. But he'd turned around and started walking back the way he'd come, and I saw no reason to correct him. I'd never see him again, and I wanted to get away from here as quickly as possible. He didn't need to know my name.

I walked down to the lake's edge, tugging my hood and mask back on as I went. It enclosed me, removing me from this space so that my breath and thoughts echoed inside. Mally had caught her infection in a river far from here, but it felt like the same polluted place, a sore on the surface of the world. It was possible to do something about it—efforts in France and elsewhere across Europe had proved that—but as usual that was all down to money. The environment agencies invested where they could, pumping funds into places that were politically expedient or where locals had enough money and clout to make enough noise. This dead lake, where old guys like the one I'd just met still lived, was being left to its fate.

Just like Mally, I thought, and the guilt bit in hard yet again. I surprised myself by gasping a sob, loud and intimate inside my protective suit. She was gone even though she was still alive, her personality eaten away and swallowed by the infection that ravaged through her body and mind. There was no cure. Treatment was now just to keep her comfortable, yet her organs struggled on, as if there was hope. It was cruel, and sometimes when I went to visit I considered pressing a pillow over her face. They would call such mercy murder.

I walked along an old concrete boat-launching ramp, unused now, and set my case down at the water's edge.

The man is limping again when he arrives back at the dock at the bottom of his garden. He walks out to the bench and sits, looks out over the lake, breathing hard. The mist has been burnt away by the sun. He can see the opposite shore. He scratches absently at the stitches in his finger, then stops and checks them. He flexes his finger a little, grunts.

After a few minutes he stands and heads back towards the house.

'Eighteen,' he says. 'Eighteen.' He repeats the word several times, as if testing its feel in his mouth, or debating whether it's right.

He does not enter the house. Instead he veers left to the large detached workshop. The door is propped open a few inches—no visitors here, no one to secure his property against—and he pulls it open on oiled hinges. He disappears inside for a while, then emerges again with something in his hand.

He rubs his knee briskly as if to impart some warmth into his aching joint, then starts walking again. The limp is lessened, and he's moving faster. As if eager.

'Eighteen,' he says again. 'That's right. That's right.'

I filled the test tubes quickly. The real testing would take place back at the lab, but two of the tubes held reactive compounds for instant, approximate readings. One showed that the lake's pH was four-point-two, almost a whole point more acidic than it had been just twelve months ago. The other showed more signs of various toxic pollutants, probably washed down from the hills to the east. There was a plastics and packaging factory several miles in that direction, and we'd been trying to take them down for years. These readings were inevitable, but they also made me sad, and mad. The lake shore was speckled with yellow foam like large mushrooms. Pebbles were bleached by the water. A few skeletal remains of large creatures were scattered here and there. They weren't fish—the last fish in this lake had died years before—but birds, mammals, and a few reptiles that had ventured or fallen into the water. They would have died quickly, I hoped. The lake was large enough to have a gentle swell when the wind blew, and some of their sad bones were eventually spat out onto the shore, stripped of flesh, fur, and scales by the toxic fluid.

I filled my sample case, snapped it shut and stood, eager to get back to the car. I was sweating inside the suit, my clothes already soaked, and the trip back to the city would be uncomfortable. I was eager to shower, because even though I was protected I still felt unclean. I wondered how much badness I'd breathed in just being here, and how that man could live close to the lake for any extended period. He was limping and looked somehow lessened. He reminded me of how Mally had looked just before she became ill.

As I crossed the car park towards my car I pushed back the helmet and unzipped my suit, letting the outside in. Even though it was warm the breeze chilled me, and I relished the feeling. I breathed softly, my own body odour smothering the chemical taint to the air, and felt the heat of the midday sun on my skin as I reached the car.

'Fuck.' I had a flat tyre. I'd been here less than thirty minutes.

'Eighteen.'

I spun around, surprised by the man's voice. He was walking towards me from the same direction as before, but this time he was pushing a wheelbarrow that contained a long metal bar with a small plastic case clipped on halfway along. There was also a heavy car jack.

'Saw your tyre,' he said. He stopped and lifted the tyre iron. 'Got a locking wheel nut set here.'

'Thanks, I…' I'd never changed a tyre in my life, and I felt a rush of gratitude. 'That's very kind.'

'No worries. Got your spare?'

I blinked, and for a few seconds my mind fluttered like a trapped bird. Mally had always said I was no good in a crisis, and she was right. I frowned at the man, looked at the car, and realised how little I knew about it.

'Probably in the boot,' he said. 'Unless it's one of those shitty tyre repair kits. If it is, your tyre is wrecked. If you're carrying a spare…' He hefted the tyre iron. It was almost as long as his leg. 'This'll do it. The irons that come with cars are never long enough.'

'Uh, yeah, thanks,' I said. 'Mind if I…?' I started stripping the protective suit, sweating more than ever. The man smiled and watched for a bit, then turned and looked back out across the lake, leaning on the metal tool.

'Used to swim in there,' he said.

'What?'

'Years ago,' he said. 'Thirty years or maybe more, when I was a kid. Even back then it was polluted, though nowhere near what it is now. They say it's how I got this.' He lifted his free hand, waved it, and ran it across his shoulder and chest without touching. I didn't know what he had, and didn't really want to ask. Now that I saw him up close I guessed perhaps some sort of wasting disease, something deep in his bones and muscles. I felt really sorry for him. He wasn't as old as I'd first thought.

I finished stripping the protective suit and rolled it up, lobbing it into the back of the car.

'I'd like to have seen it back then,' I said.

'All sorts of birds here,' he said. 'Flowers in the meadows, fish in the water, visitors through the summer and a few in the winter, too. Then we threw it all away. Tragedy, don't you think, Eighteen?'

'Truly,' I said, thinking of Mally in her bed, hooked to machines keeping her alive when she was already gone away from me. 'Davey.'

The man only nodded. 'Best check your boot.' He shifted uncomfortably, a small grimace pursing his lips.

I opened the boot and moved some of my stuff aside, grabbed the small leather tag and lifted the liner. 'Yep, it's a spare,' I said.

'Ah, great news, Eighteen,' the man said.

'It's Davey.'

I sensed the movement. Maybe it was a shadow shifting in my peripheral vision, or the day holding its breath, or the whisper of the descending tyre iron. The impact against my head sent me sprawling, and at first it felt ice-cold and blazing hot and all encompassing, yet strangely painless. I spilled to the ground, still gripping onto the car's bumper in an effort to hold myself up.

Then the pain surged in.

'There are two hundred and six bones in the human body,' the man said. 'Always good to have a spare.' He swung the tyre iron down one more time.

The man watches the car roll down the concrete boat ramp and into the lake. It tilts to one side and floats for a while, but its momentum causes it to drift out from the shore, and he's left all the doors open. Water rushes in, bubbles burst out. He waits until it's completely submerged.

It takes him a while to get the body into the wheelbarrow, but once it's done he lifts and wheels it along the broken path. By the time he reaches his house he's sweating and limping again, but he doesn't stop. He pushes it out onto the small wooden dock and dumps the body beside the bench. The tyre iron and jack fall out as well. He retrieves these, takes them and the barrow back to the workshop.

He emerges again with a length of thick steel wire looped over his shoulder. He's limping badly now, hobbling and grunting with each step. The sweat is obviously from pain as well as the physical efforts he has undertaken. He ties the cable around the bench and then the corpse's chest, sits down, and shoves the body into the lake with his feet. The splash is subdued as if poisons and pollution have thickened the water.

The man sits for a while, leaning back on his arms with his face tilted up to the sun. When he's caught his breath he stands with a lot of effort and hobbles back to his house.

He leaves the door slightly ajar. No intruders here.

Inside the house the man goes past the living room and kitchen to a small room at the rear. He stands in the doorway and sighs deeply; it seems that this is his true home.

The room is set up like an operating theatre. There's a heavy oak table in the centre, weathered hardwood darkened with blood. There's also a reclining leather chair that's similarly stained, a drip-stand to either side. Scattered around the room are various medical paraphernalia. A glass-fronted cabinet against one wall is filled with bottles and pill packets, rolled bandages and dressings, fluid-filled bags, metal bowls of varying sizes, and a wall rack on the adjacent wall holds an array of scalpels, knives, saws, drills, screwdrivers, rolled wires, metal plates of varying sizes and jars of bolts and screws. There's a tall fridge in one corner.

Three large, portable, magnifying mirrors stand on adjustable legs.

'Three,' the man says, touching his wrist.

Three was a young man whose ambition was to walk around the country raising money for environmental concerns. He stopped at the lake to write a report for his blog and social media followers. The man invited him for food, slit his throat, put him in the lake, and retrieved him seven weeks later to extract his ulna.

'Seven,' he says, running his hand across his chest. Seven was a woman travelling in an old clapped-out campervan. She camped close to the lake's car park, and when she lit a fire and started cooking the man stalked closer and shot her from twenty metres away with his crossbow. The lake swallowed her van and her body, and forty days later he hauled her out and took a rib.

'Nine.' A man driving with his son, using the time away to bond. He harvested both of their clavicles, and ended up using the man's.

'Thirteen.' A woman holidaying with her husband. Metatarsal. Unlucky thirteen.

'Seventeen.' Proximal phalanx.

The lake's water is getting more and more acidic. Seventeen

only took a little over five weeks until the remaining flesh sloughed from the skeleton when he hauled it back up onto his dock.

The man stands fast and firm against the disease which still seeks, against all his determined actions, to take him apart. He thinks Eighteen might only take a couple of weeks. He is looking forward to giving himself a new knee.

As winter closes in and there's work to do around his isolated lakeside house to prepare for this cold, hostile season, the man's gait is changing. His left side drops. He walks with a stick. It takes him half an hour to get out of bed every morning.

A few days later a woman arrives. He meets her on a walk; he continues his daily constitutionals, even though his right knee is still healing, and his left hip is now failing him. She's a bikepacker, and she says she's making the most of the late burst of autumn warmth to tour the western side of the country. Strong hips, bikers. She says her name is Belinda. He calls her Nineteen.

ABOUT THE AUTHOR

TIM LEBBON is a New York Times-bestselling writer from South Wales. He's had fifty novels published to date, and hundreds of novellas and short stories. His latest novel is *Secret Lives of The Dead*. He has won a World Fantasy Award and four British Fantasy Awards, as well as Bram Stoker, Scribe and Dragon Awards.

He's recently worked on the new computer game Resurgence, acted as lead writer on an audio drama, and he's co-writing his first comic for Dark Horse.

The movie of his novel *The Silence* debuted on Netflix in April 2019, and *Pay the Ghost* was released Hallowe'en 2015. Tim is currently developing more novels, short stories, audio dramas, and projects for TV and the big screen.

Find out more: www.timlebbon.net

BACKSLIDING

CLAY MCLEOD CHAPMAN

Mom was Mom again.

That's what Dad said. He promised me and Lela she was—*It's really her, kids, really*—swearing up and down things will go back to normal now. We just had to give her time. Be patient.

Mommy's all better, he told us, his hands placed on our separate shoulders, my right, Lela's left, a solo-parenting powwow, while keeping his eyes on Lela instead of me, as if he knew he had a better shot at convincing her than myself. Got that right. Lela's such an easy target, all six years of herself, wanting—*needing*—to believe so badly that it'd be her again, back to her old self. Good as new.

You'll see, Dad said, sounding like he was convincing himself more than either of us. *Everything'll be back to the way it was before…*

Before. Such a broken record.

The plan had been to greet her in the driveway. Lela made a sign—WELCOME HOME MOM WE LUV U—scribbled in magic marker and that new sparkly paint pen Dad bought her, a bribe, rainbow shooting stars and warped hearts scrawled across the posterboard. She'd overdone the WELCOME HOME part, so by the time she painted MOM WE LUV U, Lela really had to cram the letters together. LUV U looks like a crushed butterfly in the far right corner, its glittery wings sinking into themselves, never able to fly again.

I'd torn off the flap from an Amazon box and Sharpied MOM across it. No glitter hearts, no sparkly stars. Her name was enough, the most basic acknowledgement that this is who the sign was meant for: MOM and nobody else. Accept no substitutes. No imposters.

Dad even fastened a WELCOME BACK banner in the hallway. She'd spot it when she first walked in through the front door. We decided me and Lela would stand on the porch, wave our homemade signs when Dad pulled in. Put on a happy face. Welcome our mother back, freshly discharged, pretending everything is all hunky-dory.

But now that it was showtime, now that I could hear the crumble of gravel under tyres, I couldn't do it. I just couldn't. I ran back inside and rushed straight upstairs to my room and slammed the door. There were still scratch marks across the panelling, fingernails etched into the wood from where Mom had clawed at the door, trying to force her way in. Dad hadn't gotten around to replacing it yet, so I put a poster over it, a kitten climbing a cliff, HANG IN THERE, covering as much of the runnels as I could. A few still peeked out.

I watched from my window as Dad made his way around the car. Mom waited in the passenger side seat, staring out her own window. There were so many panes of glass between us. I felt better that way. Felt safe. There was something so empty about her eyes. Lost. She would've sat inside the car for hours if Dad hadn't opened the door for her.

As soon as he did, her eyes turned on again. Alive.

I could still make out the bruises from before. The lacerations along her face were healing from the looks of it, fading back into her flesh, but I could still see the faintest trace of scratch marks running along her cheeks. Her neck. All the spots she'd clawed at herself.

Dad held his forearm out for Mom, giving her a lift and guiding her back inside. *Easy now*, I heard him say, encouraging her to take it slow. *That's it. You got it. One step at a time.*

The last time she was here, inside our home, it had taken a massive dose of midazolam to keep her from attacking the EMT workers. I'd been the one who dialled 911. When the ambulance finally arrived, the EMTs found her still bound to her bed. She'd managed to loosen the restraint around her right wrist, the skin all raw, lashing at anyone who came near. One EMT made the mistake of getting too close. Mom raked her free hand across his face. She'd done something similar to me just a few days before. I can still hear her shrieks as the EMTs administered the midazolam, one dose, then two, enough to stun a horse, her fading shouts still bouncing throughout the house, soaking into the very walls.

That had been a month ago. I can still hear her. Every room holds its own scream, Mom's voice absorbed into the wood. The sheetrock. Our house is a sponge for her shrieks.

Dad had sat us down before heading to get her from the hospital. Time for a little pep-prep talk. We all agreed that it would be best that Dad pick her up, alone, while me and Lela stayed at home. We could welcome her back then. Get the house ready for her return. We'd cleaned up the mess from Before already by then. The shattered dishes. All the torn books. Dad hired a cleaning service to come through and give the whole house a thorough scrub-down, an entire crew of cleaners coming in to erase the blood stains out from the grout. The spiralling patterns of urine and vomit that arced across the walls, like modern art.

Dad tried to salvage the bedsheets, but the blood never came out, not fully, so he just tossed them along with everything else and bought new sheets. Fresh floral patterns. I don't think Mom will like them. They're not her style. If she'd been the one to buy them, she would've picked something simpler. A better thread count. Not that Dad listened to me. He just ordered something on Amazon and moved on, ticking off boxes on his never-ending list of how to get things back to normal. Back to the way they were Before.

I could still smell the lingering hint of iron in the air. No hibiscus-scented aroma remover could rid the floors of all that blood. That rusted penny tang clung to our home, soaked into the wood (where it jostled for space with the shrieks), the wallpaper, the very foundation of our house. It was everywhere now, a part of this place, no matter what.

We keep our windows open now. Let the sun in. Air the house out. For that last week, Before they took Mom away, the windows had been shut. Locked. Curtains closed.

Nobody knew what was happening inside here.

To us.

I'll call when we're on our way home, Dad said. *Sound like a plan?* He was asking me this, eyes on me now. Not Lela. I'm the older sister, so I'm supposed to be the responsible one. Dad wanted to make sure Mom was okay first. The two of them could have the ride back to talk. About what, I don't really know. What had happened. What will happen now.

How can we be a family now? After everything that's happened? All the things she said? *That wasn't your mother*, Dad had said so many times, that broken record skipping, caught in an endless song. *That was something else, making her say those awful things.*

Mom called me a snivelling maggot. A mistake. An abortion. She'd smiled when the words came out from her mouth, her chapped lips cracking, bleeding freely, her bloodshot eyes locked on me as she relished every sentence. The pain it caused. Savouring it all. She licked her lips, tongue flickering through the air, reaching for me, as if to lap up my tears.

It'll be tough at first, Dad told us. *Just remember: It's her. She's better. She loves you.*

The clincher: *It's still her. Still your mother.*

Such a broken record.

I had a plaster cast around my wrist that testified otherwise, but I wasn't going to bring that up now. Not after everything that's happened. I could tell Dad was just barely holding it together. He needed us to believe everything was going to be okay. Back to normal. Maybe, just maybe, if me and Lela believed it, he might begin to believe it himself.

Just give her time. It would take time to rebuild our trust. To be a family again.

Time. Trust. Patience.

Love.

Okay, Lela agreed. I think she said it because she knew that's what Dad wanted to hear. Lela hadn't seen the worst of it. The worst of her. Mom didn't throw her across the room. Didn't backhand her. Didn't sear her hand on the stove. Lela was spared all that.

We protected Lela. Shielded her. Hid her. From her own mother.

Not me so much. Nobody protected me.

From her.

MOM. That's what the posterboard said, at least.

I still wasn't so sure.

I watched as Dad guided her back inside our house. She looked so gaunt now. All hollowed out. A hundred years old. The flesh along her cheeks sunk into her jawbone, potholes at either side of her face. Craters of skin. Her eyes eased deeper into their sockets, almost like they were a pair of tiny animals afraid to peer out from the little hovels in the ground.

She had lost so much weight in the last month. She hadn't gained much back during her time in the hospital. Had she eaten anything?

I barely recognised her. My own mother.

Who was this woman?

The three of us had discussed visiting Mom while she was still in the hospital, offer her a little moral support while she was away, but Dad decided for us that it would probably be best that we didn't. He went once, by himself, right after they took her. I remember him coming back that night. It was clear to me—crystal—that he'd been crying, his eyes all red.

When Lela asked Dad why we couldn't visit her, he made up some excuse. Something the doctor said. Something about her recovery. *Blah, blah, blah*. A fib, obviously.

Dad didn't want us to see Mom that way. Remember her that way. Have the image of her all scratched up, back in her restraints, sedated into oblivion, fed through an IV-drip, eyes wide open but nobody home, jaw slack and drooling, wasting away for days while the doctors tried to figure out what had happened to her in our house. What's wrong with Mom.

If Lela saw her mom like that, the aftershocks that ravaged her body, the toll of what those men did to her in our house, Lela might never be able to see her as anything else.

Now she's back.

Good as new.

Helloooo, Dad called out as soon as he opened the door. *We're hooome…* He was trying too hard. Pretending. Acting as if this was just another day coming home from work.

I hated it.

Mom spotted us first at the top of the stairs. She had to crane her neck back to find us hovering in the upstairs hall. Lela hid behind my hip, peering out.

Hello, she said. Her voice. I recognised it. Still, it sounded flat. Distant. Medicated.

Hey, I said back, hearing the slightest scratch in my own voice.

Come on down, girls, Dad said, all business. He must've been miffed that we had already deviated from our game plan, abandoning him.

Neither of us moved.

We were all at a standstill, staring each other down, Mom and Dad at the bottom of the stairs, me and Lela at the top. The stairwell walls were covered in picture frames of us, the whole fam, back in happier times. Less possessed times. Look at us all, grinning for the pictures. Lela at three. Me in my PJs, opening a Christmas present. Dad had picked up all the broken glass from the carpeting, replacing the frames from every photo Mom had shattered with her face. I remember the web of lacerations that spread over her forehead.

That web had nearly healed now. Just the slightest pink threading of scabs branching across her scalp, weaving through her eyebrows. The bridge of her nose.

Nobody said a word. Nobody even breathed.

Mom kneeled down, right there in the hallway. She needed Dad's support to do it, using his forearm to give her enough leverage to bend one knee onto the marbled tile. Once she was down, a marriage proposal stance, she let go of Dad's arm and held out her own.

Reaching out. For us.

I missed you so much, she said, arms held out for a hug. A suspended net. A Venus flytrap. She could've held her arms open like that for hours, I imagined, a supplicating statue, waiting for one of us to wander into her embrace and that'd be that, wouldn't it?

I wasn't about to fall for it. No way, Jose. I wasn't about to budge from where I—

Lela had tiptoed out from behind me. I hadn't even noticed, so focused on Mom.

She took the first step down.

Lela, I said. I tried to grab her, yank her back, but she was already making her way down the steps, slowly at first, picking up her pace the closer to Mom she got, descending right into her open arms. I could've raced after her. I could've grabbed Lela and pulled her back up the steps, away from that trap, from Mom, but I couldn't move. Not one step.

I couldn't do it. Save my own sister.

Lela landed in Mom's embrace. I watched our mother's arms seal themselves around my baby sister, watched them slither around her neck and squeeze. Serpents at her throat. Lela was facing away from me, while Mom nestled her chin against Lela's shoulder. I couldn't see Lela's expression, but I had a clear view of Mom's. She closed her eyes. Tears sprouted out from the corners, running down each cheek. She nuzzled her lips into Lela's neck and gave her a kiss, whispering something I couldn't make out. *I love you,* maybe.

Then Mom opened her eyes to me.

Dad corralled us all into the living room. The seating

arrangement was simple: Mom sat on the couch. Dad sat next to her. He placed his hand over hers, resting in her lap.

The two of us sat on the floor. There was about two or three feet between us. Not a lot. I imagined Mom leaping off the couch and pouncing on top of me. Biting my ear again.

Dad started us off. *We're so happy to have you back, hon.*

Mom feigned a smile. Her skin was grey, a chemo complexion, as if her body had been ravaged by cancer, even though I knew that wasn't true. This hadn't been cancer.

This was something else.

Something worse.

We're going to take things slow, Dad added when nobody else spoke. Always filling in the silence. Dead air. *One day at a time. We're all in this together, as a family. Right, girls?*

Dad glanced at me. In his eyes I saw the need, the downright desperation for me—for someone, *anyone*—to back him up. Just this once. He must've been so exhausted, too.

I must've nodded, even though I don't remember moving a muscle, because he turned back to Mom with a smile of relief, as if to say, *See? Look at us. We're a team!* Dad was much better at organising our family vacations than figuring out this. Any of this.

Then again, who could? Who out there had gone through anything like this before? What family could've survived what we went through? Mom chewing on broken glass? Mom smothering me with a pillow in the middle of the night? Mom smashing Dad's head into the fridge? Mom stuffing Lela's guinea pig in the dryer and turning it on? Mom breaking my—

I just want to say, Mom started, then left it there. Her eyes drifted a bit, lips parted by a fraction, as if she were trying to remember what exactly she'd been saying. Her lips weren't as chapped as before, less flecks, but they still weren't the lips I remembered Mom having. Before. They looked rougher now, coarser somehow, thinner with dehydration.

I just want to say I'm sorry. Sorry for what I've done. What I put you two through. She paused for a moment, as if she expected us to say something. *Will… Will you forgive me?*

Lela nodded. She was ready to forgive. To forget.

Not me.

Not yet.

Now's our chance to discuss what happened, Dad said, *as a family. Do either of you have any questions that you want to ask Mommy?*

This discussion was structured for us to understand what had happened, but in reality, I knew it was something much different. This was to get our story straight. What would we tell our friends at school? The neighbours already knew something was up. How would we explain any of this to strangers who asked us? What if there were more reporters?

To lie, basically. Cover it all up.

Lela spoke first, swallowing before asking, *Are you really feeling better now?*

Mom nodded. Smiled tightly, her lips pinched. *Much better. I needed to spend some time in the hospital so the doctors could make sure I was okay. To rest.*

She was still wearing a knee brace on her left leg. I remember seeing it bend backwards. The hollow pop of her own kneecap, how it echoed throughout the kitchen.

What happened? Lela asked.

Dad was about to answer for Mom, but she flossed her fingers through Dad's hand and squeezed. I knew this was a silent signal to let her respond.

It took her a moment. *It's hard to say. I was sick. Something was wrong with me. I needed help. The things I said, the things I did… That wasn't me, okay? I swear it wasn't.*

What was it then? Lela and her million questions.

Mom thought about this. *Something got into your mother. Something made her do all those mean things. Say those awful things. I didn't want to, but… I couldn't stop myself.*

I remember the first time I noticed Mom had been acting differently. It wasn't anything earth-shattering at first. She'd be talking about something, anything, getting groceries or asking us about school—when she'd freeze—totally out of the blue. It was like somebody had pressed pause on her, Mom's body locking. Mouth open, eyes elsewhere.

It wasn't long before she was snapping at us. Growing irritable with us. There was this one dinner where I didn't clean my plate and she flung a handful of peas into my face.

Then came the scratching. Our flesh under her fingernails.

This thing was so strong, Mom said. *But… we finally got it out. It took some time, and it hurt, really hurt. So much, that even when it was over… it took a toll on my body. I just needed some time to rest. Heal. But now that it's gone and I'm better, I could come home.*

All the doctors said so, Dad added, as if having their medical seal of approval made any of this better. No mention of them. *They*. The other men who came into our house. The ones with the black and white collars. The stone-faced fellows who wouldn't speak to me.

Dad didn't want to talk about those men. Mom had been the believer way back when, even though we never would've known it. We never went to church. Didn't say grace before dinner. No prayers before bed. Now we were told to have faith in something none of us had any understanding of. No appreciation for. We were supposed to believe. In what?

Your mother and I have talked a lot about what we want to tell other people about what happened. If anyone asks you—anyone at school or any of our neighbours—you can just tell them Mommy needed to rest for a while. That she was sick and just needed to heal.

Lying. We were being asked to lie. Or almost lie. Spin the story in a different direction, away from the facts, like we were hiding a sliver of the truth. Obscuring it somehow.

Mom hadn't been herself, that's all. She'd been someone else.

Something.

I felt like we were forgetting. Moving on. It didn't feel right to be hiding from what actually happened. Even now, it felt like we were talking around it. Avoiding it.

I wasn't ready to let go. To move on and forget. Too many things had been said. Too many injuries. *Look at what you did,* I wanted to say, brandishing my cast. *Look at what you did to me. Your own daughter.*

But then I looked at Mom, the sadness in her eyes, and I could see how much she was hurting. Even now. She was so desperate for our acceptance. For our love.

Maybe it really was her.

Maybe.

The main thing is to be patient, Dad said. *It's not going to happen overnight. It'll take time. But we can do this, together, as a family. We love each other. Remember that.*

Mom took in a sharp breath and we all froze. *I just want you both to know*—she glanced at Dad—*I want you to know I love you. So much. Nothing is going to change that.*

Lela nodded. It was so easy for her. She'd accept anything Mom and Dad said.

Mom looked right at me, her eyes imploring. *Can you forgive me? Can you find it in your heart to forgive me, hon? Please?*

I remember when Mom broke my wrist. I came home from school. The house felt empty. Lela was at whatever afterschool activity she was signed up for while Dad was still at work. Most days, Mom was at home, in bed or on the couch, just resting, the television on but her attention elsewhere, her eyes on the walls or some distant space beyond, but that afternoon I couldn't find her anywhere. The house was so quiet. The TV wasn't on.

I called out for her—*Mom? You here? Mom?*—but nothing. No answer. I figured I was alone, so I wandered into the kitchen to get something to drink—and there she was. Curled on the floor. A puddle of her own urine spread out from beneath her, like the sun, a nimbus of piss. Hair flung in her face, vomit in her locks, bile lacing her cheeks in yellow streaks.

Mom? Mom—what's wrong? I raced to her, kneeling down next to her. I could hear her muttering just under her breath. I held onto her arms, trying to keep her from shaking.

It could've been a seizure. Epilepsy. Toxic—

Mom smacked me. Her hand slammed against my cheek so hard my neck bent, until my ear collided with the bulb of my shoulder.

I tried to push back, but Mom grabbed my wrist. Her grip was so tight. She reeled me in until her nose pressed against my cheek.

What a weak thing you are, she seethed through her clenched jaw. *Such a fledgling.*

Her breath smelled awful. That acrid tang of vomit.

What nimble thin bones you have, little bird, little bird, little—

She fractured my wrist. Just a simple twist and—

SNAP

—bird.

I remember those first few days when Dad didn't know what to do. He was in Damage Control Mode. He ordered a family lockdown until he could figure this all out. I'd overheard his phone calls, even when he thought nobody was listening. Always asking the same question—*What can I do? What in the hell am I supposed to do? How do I help her?*

The doctors came first. They did nothing. Saw nothing wrong.

Then came the psychologists. Or psychiatrists. I can't remember which.

Then the healers. The wellness gurus. The spiritual advisors.

Then came the other men. The men with grim expressions. When they came into our house, they wouldn't look at us. Didn't need to ask us any questions. They already knew that whatever malady Mom had couldn't be diagnosed by men of the medical profession.

They locked the door behind them, sealing me and Lela out. Dad had been paying less and less attention to us by then, so it was up to me to look after Lela. To shield her from all this. To feed her. Make sure she made it to school. That she didn't say anything.

Don't say a word about this to anyone, he whispered. *Promise me, Kyra. Nobody.*

This was a family matter. Something we had to figure out. Together.

I never felt so alone in my life.

We spent our nights in my room once the *sessions* started. Dad actually laughed when somebody said the *E*-word, so from that moment forward he simply said *sessions.*

Even though Lela had her own room, her own bed, her own stuffies and toys, she'd always sleep in mine. If there was any sleep to be had by then. The two of us would get under the covers, spooning each other. I'd wrap my arms around her from behind, holding her tight, feeling the tremble in her slender body eventually subside, sensing the very second she finally drifted off to sleep, the tension in her muscles relenting, absolutely slack. I'd stay awake, unable to fall asleep myself. Not with those men in our house. I could still hear them through the wall. All the shouting. The same refrains over and over. The shifting of furniture, as if someone were pushing the bed around, skidding across the floor.

I heard Mom laughing. Cackling in a voice that didn't sound like her.

Days of this. These sessions went on for days.

A week. All that cackling.

Shrieking.

Dad had completely forgotten about us by then. He was so preoccupied with whatever was happening in their bedroom, with those men, with Mom, that I had to fix our meals. Bathtime. Bedtime. Family time. We lived completely on our own inside our house, orphaned under our own roof, while everyone else inhabited a different time and space, two parallel existences that never ever intersected, growing further and further apart.

Sometimes, one of those men would stumble out from our parents' bedroom. Covered in sweat. Scratches. Breathless. Exhausted from the looks of it. They'd ask for water, which either me or Lela would get for them. Sometimes they'd say thanks. Most of the time, though, they didn't, simply gulping the whole glass down, catching their breath before heading back into the bedroom. Locking the door behind themselves all over again.

Just kill her, I remember thinking to myself. Maybe I even said it out loud, I don't know. A prayer. My belief. Faith. *Just let Mom die already so she can be out of her misery.*

But let's be honest with ourselves here. It wasn't Mom's misery I was hoping to end. It was ours. Mine. I'm eleven years old and all I wanted was for this to all be over. To end.

Just let her die already, let her die, let her die, let her—

Then everything went quiet. The shrieking stopped.

Someone answered my prayers. My first thought. I believed it. Truly believed. I was so relieved. I know it was wrong, but I was so relieved that this nightmare was finally over.

Finally.

Then I thought of Mom singing with a wooden spoon in the kitchen, serenading our pasta with her best Elvis impression, talking about wise men, fools rushing in.

I thought of Mom racing Dad through the Costco, me in her cart, Lela in Dad's, the four of us tearing through the aisles until we crossed the finish line.

I thought of Mom.

I thought of—

Mom.

Mom.

Mom.

I dialled 911. Called them and begged them to rescue her. *Please help her, please.*

My mother.

Please.

Save her.

Please.

Time, Dad kept echoing in the living room. *Just give it time.* That was his final word on it all. He was ready to move on. Everybody had given Mom a clean bill of health. The doctors couldn't find anything physically wrong. The scans all came back negative.

What else is there to do but heal?

We were a family again.

Reunited, at last.

I couldn't sleep.

Not with Mom back in the house. Lela was in her own bed, in

her own room, so I had the sprawl of my mattress to myself. I just lay there, on my back, staring up at the ceiling.

I strained my ears at the faintest creak throughout the house. Was that the warping of a floorboard down the hall? Was someone standing outside my door?

Where is Mom right now?

I still had my cast on for another three weeks. It itched so much. I took a pencil and slipped the tip underneath the plaster, but even then I couldn't reach the itch to scratch it.

I was desperate for a glass of water. That meant leaving my room. Heading downstairs. Could I do it? Was it safe? Out there? In the hall? Who else was out there?

I tiptoed past Mom and Dad's room. Their door was closed. Locked, probably.

I made my way down the steps, taking them one at a time, bare feet on soft carpeting, pausing long enough to listen, make sure nobody was following me.

I decided not to turn the light on in the kitchen. I didn't need it on to navigate my way through the space, blindly opening the cabinet and grabbing a glass.

I decided I wanted orange juice instead of water.

I opened the door to the fridge. The light from inside reached across the kitchen.

Mom was sitting at the table. The light found her face.

Silent. Unmoving. Staring back at me.

How long had she been sitting there? In the dark? Not saying anything?

. . . Mom?

Hey, hon, she said. All sun. *Guess I'm not the only one who couldn't sleep, huh?*

Are . . . are you okay? I wanted to call for Dad. Call 911. Call anyone.

I'm fine. Just a little anxious, I guess... You?

I'm fine, I managed to say, then swallowed.

It's okay if you're not. This must be really hard on you. You more than most.

I didn't say anything. But it's true. I did feel that way.

I don't expect you to forgive me, hon. I don't know if I'd be able to if I were in your shoes... I just want you to know that. That I understand. You can be mad at me. It's okay.

I didn't say anything. I just listened.

But I'm going to try. I'm going to try very, very hard to earn your trust back. Your love.

I heard her sniffle. I realised I hadn't closed the refrigerator door yet. Dad would've scolded me for leaving it open, letting all the cool air out, wasting electricity, but if I shut it, there would be no light in the kitchen, nothing to illuminate my mother's face, the faintest trace of scabbed webbing still spread across her forehead, her nose, her cheeks. Her eyes.

I didn't want to be in the dark, alone, with her.

There is nothing I want more in this world, she said. *Your love.*

I saw her bring her hand up to her face, wiping her cheek.

Nothing in this world...

Now I saw them. All the tears. Mom was crying.

I know you were the one who called the ambulance. If it weren't for you, I don't think—I don't think I'd be here now. You saved my life, sweetie. Saved me.

Mom. My mom.

Thank you, she said, wiping everything away. All the tears. *Thank you...*

I took a step toward her. Just a small one. Mom hesitated, almost recoiled—from me—the moment she realised what I'd done. Her breath caught in her lungs. Held onto it.

Mom? I asked. Truly asked.

Mom nodded. *It's me,* she said and raised her arms. I could see how much of an effort it took to lift them. All her strength. There'd be nothing left. But she did it. For me.

So I took another step. Then another.

Into her arms.

Oh, Kyra…

I felt her arms slowly close around me, felt them slide over my back, her hands twining at my sides, slithering against my hips, bringing me in closer, closer, her face now at my shoulder, chin rooting itself into the clavicle at my neck. I felt her breath, the heat of it.

Darling. Her voice at my ear. Lips at the lobe.

Then she squeezed.

ABOUT THE AUTHOR

CLAY MCLEOD CHAPMAN is the author of novels *What Kind of Mother, Ghost Eaters, Whisper Down the Lane, The Remaking, Wake Up and Open Your Eyes*, as well as various short stories and middle grade series.

Quiet Part Loud, a 12-part horror podcast from Jordan Peele/ Monkeypaw Productions, written by Chapman and Mac Rogers, is available on Spotify.

His work has been adapted into award-winning films, including *The Boy* (SXSW 2015), a feature-length adaptation of *Henley,* co-written with director Macneill, was produced by SpectreVision (Elijah Wood, Daniel Noah, and Josh C. Waller) in 2015.

In comics, Chapman is the writer of the Marvel series *Scream: Curse of Carnage*. He has written *Absolute Carnage: Separation Anxiety*, *Iron Fist: Phantom Limb, Typhoid Fever*, as well as for *Edge of Spider-Verse* and *Venomverse*, *The Avengers, Amazing Spider-Man, Ultimate Spider-Man, American Vampire*, *Scream: King In Black,* and *ORIGINS* among others. He is the creator of *Self Storage* (451 Media) and *Lazaretto* (BOOM! Studios).

Chapman is the creator of the rigorous storytelling session The Pumpkin Pie Show. In the twenty years of its existence, it has performed internationally at the Romanian Theatre Festival of Sibiu, Edinburgh Fringe Festival, New York International Fringe Festival, Winnipeg Fringe Festival, Edmonton Fringe Festival, Minnesota Fringe Festival, Dublin-based thisisnotashop art space, IGNITE Festival, Women Center Stage Festival and Impact Theatre Festival.

Chapman was educated at the North Carolina School of the Arts for Drama, the Burren College of Art, and Sarah Lawrence College. He currently teaches writing at The Actors Studio MFA Program at Pace University. He lives with his family in New York.

ACKNOWLEDGEMENTS

Lisa Tuttle: *It Gets Everywhere*, copyright © 2025 by Lisa Tuttle

Ally Wilkes: *Drop Shock*, copyright © 2025 Ally Wilkes

Lily Kade: *Muses*, copyright © 2025 by Lily Kade

Adrian Tchaikovsky: *Ghost Hunt*, copyright © 2025 by Adrian Tchaikovsky

T.L. Huchu: *The Midnight Burn*, copyright © 2025 by T.L. Huchu

V. Castro: *The Butcher of Puckley Village*, copyright © 2025 by V. Castro

Olivie Blake: *Tell Me I'm Scrumptious*, copyright © 2025 by Olivie Blake

Ramsey Campbell: *The Compensation*, copyright © 2025 by Ramsey Campbell

Rian Hughes: *The Other Brother*, copyright © 2025 by Rian Hughes

Lindy Ryan: *Stay in Touch*, copyright © 2025 by Lindy Ryan

Susi Holliday: *Mr Perfect*, copyright © 2025 by Susi Holliday

Tim Lebbon: *Bow Knee Lake*, copyright © 2025 by Tim Lebbon

Clay McLeod Chapman: *Backsliding*, copyright © 2025 by Clay McLeod Chapman